the
ringleader

sneha roy

Leadstart
INKSTATE

ISBN: 978-93-89759-55-6
© Sneha Roy, 2020
Cover Design: Ashwini Jadav
Layout: Ashwini Jadhav
Printing: Thomson Press

Published in India 2020 by
INKSTATE BOOKS
An imprint of
LEADSTART PUBLISHING PVT LTD
Unit 25/26, Building A/1, Wadala (East),
Mumbai 400 037, Maharashtra, INDIA
T + 91 96 99933000 **E** info@leadstartcorp.com
W www.leadstartcorp.com

Dedication

For my grandfathers, Dadai and Bata,
who gave me their love of writing and literature.

About the Author

Sneha is currently a high school student and has been writing poems and short stories since the age of 5. This is her first attempt at a novel. A trained pianist and guitarist, her other passions include French, Economics and travel.

Acknowledgements

As I wrap up the incredible journey of writing this book, several thank yous are in order.

First, to my dad, for the constant encouragement and inspiration, without which I would have never begun to write this book. Thank you for being the kindest critic, and for believing in a story I wrote when I was 10.

My mum, without whom I would have never finished this book, and for the endless supply of snacks. Thank you for staying up for the late nights, and waking up for the early mornings.

My sister, my first editor, who had to answer hundreds of questions that began with "Hey do you think this sounds cool?"

My friends, for being my first readers. Thank you for reading my poems and stories over the years, and for pretending they were all good.

My teachers, in both Malaysia and India, for helping my writing style evolve over the years and for letting me experiment in my English tests- even if that meant going over the word limit.

I'm incredibly grateful to mentor from Chennai, for teaching me the many nuances of writing and for helping me look at my characters in a new light.

A special thanks to Malini Nair and editors Sita Bhaskar, Jayati Sarkar and Rajeshwari Kejriwal of LeadStart Publishing for their valuable feedback and for guiding me through this process for the first time.

Thank you to everyone at Leadstart Publishing for being incredibly accommodating with my exam schedules and for supporting me on this journey.

And last but by no means least, a huge thanks to you, the reader, for giving this book a chance.

Prologue

Anthony Garcia

Rio de Janeiro

Brazil

The streets of Complexo de Alemao still glistened with droplets of blood from last night's fight. Mosquitoes were infesting the half-dried pools of blood, while wild stray dogs lurked in the shadows, their hungry mouths open wide. People stepped over rivulets of blood hurriedly and went along their way. From balconies above, women shouted down to vendors, while others hung clothes to dry, turning a deaf ear to the wailing noises in the background from grieving families, who had lost loved ones in the fights from the night before. Luca's gang had brutally beaten Raoul to death, the son of a store owner. He had been caught smuggling cocaine out of the house by his father. If there was any rule that came with being part of a gang, it was that you never got caught. No matter what happened, you always had to get away with it. Every single time.

Suddenly, there was the purr of an expensive automobile. Heads turned as a sleek black Mercedes came into view; like that of a panther, stalking its prey. Adults hurriedly got out of the way, averting their eyes; grungy, tattooed teens glared suspiciously at the car, wondering whether it was a new gang leader, or a drug lord. The car drove past slowly. In it, sat a man in an expensive Armani suit and sunglasses. He often took this detour, the commotion and the violence a grisly reminder of the person he used to be. He raised his hand to his face, fingers grazing over an age-old scar. *So little had changed.*

The car rolled out of the neighbourhood, and made its way back towards the main city. Crumbling cement was soon replaced by the beginning of a concrete jungle, as the car crossed boulevards and avenues before coming to a stop in front of a single building. The building was an architectural splendour. It had been constructed with the idea of building blocks in mind. The building looked like boxes precariously placed on top of one another, with wide gaps in between. Carmen Industries was printed in bold on the side of the topmost box. Under it, in smaller letters, the words 'Rio de Janeiro' were neatly printed. The car smoothly made its way to the front entrance, where it stopped. A chauffeur stepped out of the driver's seat to open the door for his boss.

Anthony Garcia stepped out, his face dark as thunder, his eyebrows furrowed in anger, his lips fixed in a thin line. What he had just been told had been ominous. He had just been nudged out of a multi-million-dollar deal by an extremely important client, who had chosen to align themselves with the very company that had recently dislodged Carmen Industries from the number 1 spot in India. CooperCoal. Garcia- a man who had fought his way out of the slums to wealth and power- immediately knew where he was headed next. He spoke into his phone- "Dube, I'm flying in."

1

Maia

The bright rays of a new day streamed through the windows, each particle struggling to get in front of the other. They focused on the frame of a young girl, sprawled on her bed, her pillows thrown aside. Her dark brown hair was knotted at the top of her head, loose strands falling around her face. Her face suddenly twisted, lips withering in distaste, as her alarm rang, waking her up from her perfect trance. She threw off her light blue duvet and stomped her way to the bathroom, muttering angrily on the way. No matter what day it was- regardless of the fact that it was Saturday, regardless of the fact that this was her second last day of freedom before school started again, her parents insisted that she wake up at six every morning. She quickly brushed her teeth, and changed into her running clothes. She went running every morning, a habit inculcated a few years ago by her parents. She usually didn't mind, but on the days like this, when everyone was probably still asleep- she minded. She ran out of the bathroom, whipping her hair up into a ponytail. She opened her drawer and fished out her old iPod. She had just recently lost her phone at school, and hadn't had the time to stock the new one with any songs yet. She hurried downstairs, still blinking the sleep away from her eyes and stepped out.

She loved the way her house looked early in the morning, the first rays of sunlight coming through the canopy of trees above. It gave the brownstone houses a certain shine that made them look even grander than they actually were. Her house was sandwiched between two others, with just a wide lawn separating them from the narrow road that snaked its way in between the houses. On the other side, there were a host of trees along with several benches where Maia often sat and studied. She walked until the footpath, and began jogging. The cool Bangalore breeze hit her in the face- effectively waking her up. The path was empty this morning, except for the occasional elderly couple out for an early morning walk. She waved to most of them and stopped to have a chat with a few, having known them since she was little. She had lived on the same street for ten years, and had watched the whole area grow. She could navigate the entire place with her eyes closed, and had done so many times in her childhood. There were fifteen Victorian-style houses, built side by side, each with its very own backyard and front yard. It had been built in the late 1800s and to this day, still stood tall and proud against the onslaught of time.

The morning breeze helped her clear her head, and also reminded her of her senior project. The whole grade was required to write an essay based on a single word or phrase. They had been given the project two months ago, and Maia had made no progress on it at all. She had relentlessly looked through every dictionary she could find for a word that would determine her happiness on graduating, but hadn't found the perfect one yet. She needed something substantial, something that she could channel her emotions through. But she came up with nothing. Every word looked pale and mundane, printed on the page without a second thought. Nothing made her want to look more.

Thirty minutes later, she ran down the path one last time, before re-entering her house, beads of sweat making their way down her forehead, and into her eyes, making them burn. Unlike the exterior of the house, which was like a travel back in time, the interior was entirely different. It had been designed in a contemporary style. The whole house had white, white-based, blue or steel coloured furniture with modern art hung on the walls, bringing vibrancy to the house. All of the art pieces had been picked up at exhibitions from around the world. She walked into the kitchen for a quick snack, and was greeted by her parents. Her mother was making something in a large bowl, and her father was on his laptop.

"How was your run?" he asked, not looking up.

"Good," she replied. "I met some of the neighbours. Did you know that Varun is moving to the US for college next year?"

"Oh, yes his mother told me about it!" her mother said. "Doesn't that make you excited? You're almost 18! This is going to be such a new exciting chapter in your life! I remember when I was about to graduate." She smiled to herself.

Maia chuckled. "So, then you also remember the insurmountable stress and academic burden that comes along with it?"

Her father nodded, a nostalgic smile playing across his face. "It'll all be worth it. Trust me." He stood up and retrieved a package from under the island table. It was a flat box covered in bright red wrapping paper, with a gold bow stuck in the middle.

Maia squealed. "Is that a present for me?"

"Well, it sure does say 'to Maia' on it. If that means you, then I think yes, it is yours." Her mother laughed. She pushed it towards Maia, as she sat excitedly on the table. She shook it gently, trying to guess what it was. After a few seconds, she gave up and gently began to open it. As the logo on the box came into view, she screamed in delight.

"Oh, thank you thank you thank you!" She gushed, clutching a brand-new laptop tightly to her chest, cradling it like it was a newborn baby.

"Do you like it? It's the latest model," her mother said.

"Oh, I love it! I love it so much! As a matter of fact, I was just looking at this laptop a few days ago! It has the coolest features. You guys are the best. But why such an expensive gift all of a sudden?" Maia asked.

"No specific reason," her father said, but didn't meet her eye.

Instantly Maia's mind flashed back to the dozens of times this had happened before. Her last laptop had come into her possession a similar way.

"Which one is this for," she asked quietly, biting her lip. "Your absence at the sports meet or the band performance?"

Her mother laughed nervously, and waved her hand around the air. "Come on," she said. "This is almost a rite of passage present. You're going to be a part of a certain lifestyle soon. You'll finally start learning about the company at eighteen like you promised, and that old box just wouldn't do!"

Maia's heart sank. She had been telling them for years, but they never understood. She wasn't interested in business. She quite frankly didn't care. She quietly put the laptop back on the table. "I'm going to take a shower," she muttered and turned around to head towards her room, when her mother called her back.

"Wait, Maia, don't just leave like that. It's a little rude," her mother said, her tone turning stern.

Maia huffed and sat back down. "I'm not interested in business," she said softly. "I don't want to do it. I know how much your company means to you and the struggle you've had to face to get it to where it is now, but I can't do it. I'm sorry, I can't. I've told you this before, and I'll keep telling you until you finally understand."

"We know, Maia. But it wouldn't hurt to just give it a try would it? Who knows, maybe you'll end up loving it. Things are a lot different from what you learn in school as a subject. Just because you don't enjoy it at school doesn't mean you won't like it in reality," her mother said.

Tears welled up in Maia's eyes, and she stood up again. "I will be taking my shower now." She ran up the stairs two at a time and rushed into her room, banging the door shut behind her.

Her room was on the first floor. Unlike the rest of the house, her room had colour at every inch. Her bed was opposite the door, and was loaded with pillows of all different shapes, sizes and colours. Maia sank down to the floor behind the door, pressing the balls of her palms into her eyes. Phosphenes danced in her eyes, as she blinked. On the wall behind her bed, were a host of Polaroid pictures, stuck on her wall in the shape of a heart. A small smile played on her face, as she looked at each of the photos, taken with friends, family, classmates, and on holidays. As her eyes came to rest on a specific picture, her smile faltered a bit, and her eyes lost their sparkle. *Tanya. My best friend or my best enemy?*

Suddenly, Maia didn't want the holidays to end. She didn't want to return to school. Or more specifically, return to Tanya.

✳

Tanya

They say that being rich means being happy. If there was anyone who could object to that, it would be Tanya. She desperately tried to find something appealing in all of the luxuries her life handed to her on a silver platter, but everything seemed drab and grey to her. She was staring at her wall, in the midst of a major pity party. Her wall was a dark blue, with small plants winding up in light blue. She had stared at this wall for as long as she could remember. Over the years, several photographs had begun to border the walls- the newest one being her school principal handing her gold medal at the State Cycling Championships. This wall had her deepest fears, highest hopes, and loudest cries etched into them. She suddenly felt an odd and sticky wetness on her palm. She carefully uncurled her palm, wincing with pain. Her hand had deep red blood splattered across it, and in the middle, sat a gold earring. Her mother's gold earring. She had been holding it so hard, that the end had cut deep into her skin. *How did this get here? I haven't even been to her room today.* She quickly stood up and strode to her bathroom before she could be caught with it. She cleaned her hand and quickly slapped a band-aid on to it. She then washed the gold earring in case any blood had got on it. As she exited the bathroom, she heard footsteps coming towards her room. She quickly sat on her bed and opened a drawer to put the earring in. The drawer was filled with things, none of which she could call her own. There was a jewel embedded mirror that belonged to her mother, and several pairs of cuffs that belonged to her father. *How did these even get in here? What's happening to me?* She heard the doorknob turn, and quickly threw the earring into the drawer and turned around. A tall, slender male figure walked in, his hair flopping over his huge glasses, covering most of his eyes. Her brother.

"Ma says if you don't come down now, your dinner will get cold," he said, raking his fingers through his hair in a futile attempt to hold it back.

"Ma also says you should get a haircut, but I don't see that happening either," she said, not bothering to look at her brother.

"Come on Tanya, don't be difficult. We're all trying to adjust here," Nikhil replied, walking over and sitting on her bed.

"Difficult? Is that how she put it?" Tanya tried not be difficult. In fact, she tried very hard not to be anything at all. But it was hard not to be jealous from time to time. Wouldn't anyone be, if they had a genius brother who was invited to speak at TED talks, host workshops at schools, and to even meet the Prime Minister?

Exasperated, Nikhil stood up to leave the room. "Just come down in a while yeah? You're going to leave soon. Don't leave on a bad note." With that, he walked out.

She couldn't wait to leave. Every time she came back to Delhi on break, she clung on to the little hope she had left, that maybe this time, things could be different. She was proved wrong every single time. The drawer on her bedside table caught her attention again. She pulled it open, and stared at its contents. Apart from things belonging to her parents, there were some items that she had never seen before. They definitely didn't belong to her family, and they most probably didn't belong to anyone in her current school either. Looking at them, she suddenly remembered an incident from two weeks ago.

She recalled an extreme amount of anxiousness, the kind that lit a fire at the pit of your stomach. She had walked into her parent's room. She remembered seeing her father's diamond suit cuffs lying on the bedside table, in a way that made her feel challenged. They had lain there, without any protection. The sudden question of 'will I be caught?' intoxicated her, and the only thing she could do was find out. She had walked towards the cuffs, and found the anxiety coming back to her again. Without a second glance to see if anyone was looking, she snatched the cuffs from their place on the dresser, and shoved them into the pocket of her jeans. As soon as she had felt the cuffs through the pocket of her jeans, a feeling of pure euphoria engulfed her in its grasp. She felt pure joy, and a strange sense of accomplishment. Later that night, she had heard her father frantically looking for it, but she didn't care.

Now, looking at it in her drawer, she felt gutted. She was too guilty to put it back, because her father would surely notice it, back after so long. He would undoubtedly turn to Tanya, thinking she was the one to blame. She rolled them in her hands, deciding what to do with them, when her door suddenly flew open, to reveal her mother. She looked at Tanya, and then at Tanya's hands. Her eyes narrowed at the sight of the cuffs.

"Where did you get those?" she enquired. Then, walking towards Tanya and seeing the contents of the open drawer, her confused expression turned to one of pure rage. "Why are these in your room? We've been looking for these for ages! You took them, didn't you?" she asked, fingering her gold earrings.

"Why would I do that?" Tanya retorted, when her mother put her hand in the air, motioning for her to stop.

"I thought all of this had stopped when we moved you out of your school here. You always wanted to cause the most trouble possible to disrupt this family from its place. The whole point of getting you away from here was so that this stupidity would come to an end." her mother said.

"So this would stop'? This isn't new to you! I've done this before?" Tanya's voice raised with every word, anger colouring her speech.

"Of course, I knew! What do you think got you expelled from your last school? You're a kleptomaniac!" Her mother spat. "I've had enough of this nonsense. You're going back tomorrow."

"They kicked me out? What happened to spending more time on Nikhil? While I suppose that has always been true, do you really think I was too weak to handle the truth?" Tanya's anger had blocked her ears, with a ringing noise, causing her to completely ignore the last part of the sentence.

With one last glare, her mother left the room, but not before she dipped her hand into the drawer and took out what belonged to her and her husband. "I came here to tell you to come down and get your food, but I guess if you need some you can go down and take some for yourself."

As soon as the door closed shut, Tanya felt the tears start to fall. In a minute, she was sobbing, her shoulders shaking. She pressed the balls of her palms to her eyes, in an attempt to stop the tears. Normally, in a situation like this, she would call Maia. But now, she wasn't so sure she could. They hadn't left off before the break on the best terms, and Tanya wasn't sure she had the liberty to call Maia. Anyhow, she picked up her phone and clicked on Maia's number.

"Hello?" Maia's voice came through, immediately calming Tanya's nerves.

"Hey Maia. It's Tanya," she replied hesitantly.

"Yeah, I figured. Are you okay?" Maia said.

Relief coursed through Tanya's nerves. No matter how angry Maia was at Tanya, she still cared for her best friend. "I'm not exactly sure. You remember the school I went to here in Delhi?"

"Yeah, what about it?"

"Well turns out, they kicked me out."

"What? Why?"

Tanya's voice lowered into a whisper. "Apparently I'm sick in the head. A kleptomaniac."

There was a chilling silence for a moment. Neither girl said anything and both waited for the other to say something.

"Do you think I'm a freak? I don't steal things any more, I don't think so. I swear. I'm pretty sure I haven't done anything since I joined the school in Bangalore." Tanya knew she was lying to Maia, but what else was there to do? And it wasn't even like Maia would get to know anyway.

"Of course, I don't think you're a freak." Maia reassured her. "So, what are you going to do now, I mean in terms of getting yourself better?"

"I don't know, I haven't thought that far ahead, I'm coming to Bangalore tomorrow anyway." Tanya said.

"But weren't you supposed to return next week?"

"I guess my mum doesn't want me to miss school." Tanya was lying through her teeth, and she realised she liked it. She liked making up stories, fabricating the truth.

Maybe she could do it more often.

✳✳✳

The sound of the doorbell resonated through the house, as Tanya's mother rushed to get it. Tanya fidgeted with her dress, pushing her hair behind her shoulders for what felt like the hundredth time. People around her milled about with champagne glasses in their hands, too engrossed in their own conversations to notice her. She stood up and stretched her legs a little, wobbly in her heels. She took them off and set them next to a small table. Her mind still felt uneasy, as it had been since the start of the day. She kept drumming her fingers against her thighs, and constantly felt like she was spiralling. She walked towards the grand staircase of her house, pushing past men in tuxedos and women in elegant sarees and gowns.

There was a large banner to her right that said, 'Congratulations Nikhil!' She tried to, but could not remember what it was he had done. She lifted her dress up, running up the staircase. She passed by her brother's room, and did a double stop. She crept in and closed he door behind her. She was sweating, even though the air conditioning was turned on. She padded around the room in her bare feet, unsure of what she was looking for. She felt a strange feeling at the pit of her stomach, as she moved towards her brother's desk. She opened his second drawer, and took out his stapler. The heavy weight of the stapler calmed her and she stopped spiralling. She rushed out of his room, tightly clutching his stapler. She entered her room, and put it on her desk, next to her own stapler. She returned to the party feeling giddy with happiness, her hands still hot from the feeling of accomplishment.

2

Mahesh Dube

Dube never left the house without his daily puja. The days he accidentally did, were bound to be terrible. Very much like this one.

He had been running late, something that usually never happened. His hair still matted against his forehead in a wet, tangled mess, he said a quick goodbye to his mother and headed out of the house. He should have been out at least 45 minutes ago. To make matters worse, his boss had flown in from Brazil the night before. The elevator made a sound, signalling its presence on his floor. As soon as it opened, he rushed inside - only to find the elevator packed with people, and the overweight button glowing an alarming red. With a frustrated sigh, Dube backed out of the elevator, and watched the doors close. He eyed the stairs, and considered taking the long walk down, but a sharp pain in his leg and the crutch resting against his waist reminded him otherwise. Stairs didn't pity the crippled.

The next elevator dinged open, thankfully empty. Dube hobbled in and as the elevator went down, he whipped out his phone. There were several messages, all from the same person.

6:30 a.m.

From: Anthony Garcia

Urgent meeting @ 9. Meet me at my office at 8:30 to go over a few important points first.

8:30 a.m.

From Anthony Garcia

What part of 'meet me at my office at 8:30' do you not get?

Dube began to reply - I'm sorry I don't control the city, but then quickly deleted it. He shook his head. He was weak, and he knew it.

Others knew it as well. Right from his days at school, Dube had been overshadowed by those seemingly 'above' him in the social hierarchy of popularity. His age had been a huge disadvantage as well. He'd been incredibly smart as a child, but hadn't been able to go to school until the age of ten. On giving the admission test in school, he was immediately admitted into the 7th grade, along with a fully paid scholarship from the government. Due to his extreme intelligence and young age, Dube would often find himself having to bring home his homework along with the homework of about a dozen others as well.

Resigned, Dube texted Garcia saying he would be there in about fifteen minutes. Dube was now in his car, and was being driven to his office. Although he had a driver for about six years now, he still couldn't get used to the fact that he could actually afford a driver- let alone a car.

In comparison to the Rio de Janeiro office, the Bangalore office of Carmen Industries was quite unostentatious. It was one tall building, flanked by several other buildings. His car smoothly rolled through the large gates and stopped in front of the main gate. He stepped out, straightening his tie and suit jacket at the same time. As he walked in through the gates, briefcase in hand, he heard several calls of 'Good morning, sir' and 'Have a good day, sir'. As he walked into the main building, he fought to keep his smile to himself.

***

A tall, well-dressed man loomed above Dube's mere five and a half feet. He shifted his weight from one foot to the other- uncomfortable by the man's mere proximity. He looked at the maid cleaning the room, and for a second wished he was the one cleaning the room, and not facing Garcia.

"Mr. Garcia." Dube said, setting his briefcase on the floor. At the man's order, he took a seat, and set his hands on the table, bracing himself.

"A hello or good morning would have been just as good, but maybe things work differently here?" Garcia said with a light chuckle.

Dube kept silent- unsure whether his boss was being sarcastic or not.

"So, you don't do replies either? Let's get straight to business, shall we?" Garcia paused for a moment and took a deep breath and continued, his tone opposite to what it was just a second ago. "So, I assume you've heard about our current situation?" Garcia paused for a second and looked at Dube.

Dube nodded.

"It can't last. We need to get back to where we were before. And fast."

"Do you have a plan?" Dube inquired.

Garcia smirked in reply. "I always have a plan." He reached into his bag and took out his laptop. He opened it and turned it towards Dube. There was a picture of a family. Parents, with a young girl between them. As Dube looked closer, he felt a tiny and familiar ball of fear in his stomach, but fought it down.

"That's the couple that owns CooperCoal."

"Good job."

"Why are you showing me this?"

Garcia pointed towards the young girl in the picture.

"That is who we need," he said firmly. "That's the centre of their life. Their daughter. That's who we make disappear, and that's who brings back our glory."

3

Maia

"Ramesh! We're going to be late! I don't want to be late on my first day back!" Maia yelled into the garage, as she tapped her foot impatiently on the hard, concrete ground. Her backpack was slung over her shoulder, and she was pulling on her tight ponytail.

"One second madam! The car isn't starting!" Came a voice from inside, and Maia heard the sound of an engine. She heaved a sigh of relief and climbed into the car as soon as it pulled up. She slid in, careful not to ruin her recently ironed uniform. She plugged her earphones in, and closed her eyes, laying her head back for a quick nap.

She woke up to her driver- Ramesh, shaking her awake. "We're here madam. You must get up now, or you'll get tardy," he said.

Maia rubbed her eyes, plucked her earphones out of her ears and stepped out of the car. She waved a quick goodbye to Ramesh, and headed through the large gates of East Hill Academy.

The entrance was a maze of black and white coloured plaid. Maia scanned the crowd for any familiar faces.

"Maia! Over here! How was your break?! I haven't seen you in absolutely ages! How've you been?!" Maia's breath was suddenly knocked out of her, when someone suddenly hugged her a little too enthusiastically. Without even looking, Maia knew exactly who she was hugging back.

"Shanaya! Hi, hey," Maia said, struggling to detach the girl from her tight grasp.

Shanaya let go, and began to nervously giggle. "Sorry! I'm just so happy to see everyone after break." The girl flushed again, and stepped back. Shanaya, was, in many ways, just like a puppy. She ran around you, and had an annoying cuteness to her that one couldn't not like.

"It's okay, really. Have you by any chance seen Tanya? I really need to talk to her. It's kind of important." Maia looked at Shanaya hopefully.

Shanaya nodded enthusiastically and pointed in the general direction of the massive building behind them.

"She's in her dorm. She came yesterday. Word's going around that she hasn't been out since then. She skipped dinner and everything," Shanaya said, before waving a quick goodbye to Maia, and scuttling off to greet her other friends. Maia froze. *She hasn't been out for almost a day? What if...?* With a vigorous shake of her head, Maia dismissed the thought from her head. She assured herself that Tanya was okay, and ran towards the direction of the dormitories.

East Hill Academy had a Tudor-style architecture, the brown stone gleaming like copper against the sun. The central building resembled a church with a clock tower. It was 7:45 AM She had exactly 45 minutes to find Tanya. She ran into the building with the dormitories, and swiped herself in. She shoved her card into her pocket and made her way up to Tanya's room on the second floor. Most dorms were shared, but Tanya's parents wanted her to have one specifically for herself, and had paid a lot extra for a private room. She even had a bathroom to herself. Maia had always wondered why, but didn't want to be nosy. Now, Maia suspected it was because of Tanya's kleptomania. Since Tanya's phone call two days ago, Maia hadn't thought about their conversation much. She didn't know how she was to take the news of her best friend being an unintentional thief. Tanya said she had never stolen anything after she had moved to Bangalore, but how could Maia believe her? That phone call had been their first and last conversation over the whole duration of their four-day break. They had left off on a fight, and Maia wasn't sure if they were to pretend as if though nothing had happened.

She stopped in front of Tanya's door and was about to knock, before stopping herself. She debated going back and waiting for class to start, but what if something happened by then? She refused to think of the possibilities, but who knew? It could happen. And if Maia could stop it before it happened, she had to. She hesitantly knocked six times on the door. Six knocks let Tanya know that Maia was at the door. After a few seconds, she heard a voice call, "Come in!"

Maia pushed the door open, and was greeted to the sight of Tanya's back. She was meticulously placing things inside her side bag, while trying to keep her hair from untying at the same time.

"Um...hi," Maia said nervously.

At this, Tanya turned around and gave her a tired smile. She was dressed in the school uniform- a white shirt, a black plaid tie and skirt- but looked dishevelled. Clothes were strewn across the floor, and the several medals and trophies Tanya had received from cycling competitions lay all over. Her shirt was crumpled with the buttons done all wrong, and the tie was about to fall out of its knots. Maia's eyebrows furrowed in worry at this sight. What had happened to her? Tanya laughed flippantly. "Don't mind my uniform, I'm going to change out of it. I think I might have slept in it."

"You think? You don't know?" Maia asked her, her mind racing ahead and jumping to several conclusions at once. She scanned the room in case she found any bottles, but, thankfully, saw none.

"I got here in the afternoon, and then set up my room till late in the night. I think I fell asleep in the process. Just give me a minute, I'll go and change," Tanya said picking a stack up neatly folded clothes.

"But Tanya, day before yesterday..." Maia started to say, when Tanya averted her eyes.

"I'll be back in a minute. Just wait here, we can walk together to the language building then yeah?" Tanya said quickly backing into the bathroom. Before the door could close, something fell out of the pile of clothes.

Maia walked over and bent down to pick it up to give it to her. She stopped in her tracks, eyes scanning the object with a flicker of recognition. It was her old phone. The one Maia thought she had lost. She turned it in her hands treating it as if it was a dangerous weapon. *Why would it be here? I lost it months ago. But you lost it here, right here, at school.* A small voice at the back her of her head said. *Maybe it was never lost. It was just stolen. All this time, while you went frantic with worry looking for it everywhere, it was right there, in the bag of the very person who was helping you look for it. She was lying. All this time.* Maia tried to fight the voice down, ashamed at herself for blaming her best friend so quickly. But there was that thing from the other day.

You know it was her. Everything the voice said was true. And there was nothing Maia could possibly do to change it. She quickly switched the device on urgently tapping her foot, in a hopeless attempt to make it switch on faster- and was relieved to see that the password was still the same. With her fingers crossed, Maia went to the contacts list to see if it had been used since she had lost it. She silently prayed that it hadn't, because that would mean that Tanya had found it somewhere. That was the only way it could have been, because apart from Maia herself, Tanya was the only one who had known the phone password.

Maia's heart sank. Since September- the month she had lost it, several calls had been made. Amongst the various numbers, Maia recognised one of them as Tanya's mother. The bathroom doorknob turned. She quickly switched the phone off and sat on the edge of Tanya's bed hoping to look as if though she hadn't moved.

Tanya walked in, looking refreshed, in a different uniform. Seeing the small smile directed at her, Maia heart lurched with a sudden wave of anger. She stood up, her lip curling in disgust.

"You know, of all the things I thought you were, I never gave you credit for being a liar," Maia spat angrily.

Tanya's eyes immediately went down to Maia's hand, where the phone was held. Her face morphed into a mask of shame. "Maia I..."

"Save it. I don't want to hear it." Maia got up, and threw the phone onto the bed. "And you know what? Keep the phone. Think of it as somewhat of an early birthday present. Oh, and find yourself a new seat in class. The one next to me won't be so inviting anymore."

"Wait! Maia! Stop! I swear I've changed!"

Ignoring her, Maia picked up her backpack from the floor and left the room, closing the door with a loud bang. She reached the end of the corridor and let out a frustrated sigh. She kicked the wall in front of her in hopes of relieving some of her anger, but instead grimaced, as a surge of pain shot up her leg, temporarily blinding her. She threw herself on the floor, and cradled her injured foot in her hands. She looked at her watch. She had twenty minutes to get to class. With her hand on the wall, Maia picked herself up from the floor, and made her way to the stairs. She clenched her teeth to keep herself from screaming on every step. She reached the end of the staircase and staggered to the main hallway and exited the building.

East Hill Academy consisted of several buildings scattered along 15 fifteen acres of land. Each building was about two or three stories and each of them served a specific purpose. Maia made her way to the language block, where her first class for the day was. Lucky for Maia, her classroom was on the ground floor. She hobbled in, determined to not let her friendship problems get in the way of her education.

***

The school bell rang, signifying the end of yet another exhausting day and the beginning of the long weekend. Maia grabbed her English books and stuffed them into her bag. She looked over at Tanya. Her head was pillowed in her arms, and she was snoring softly. Maia's eyes narrowed and she huffed in frustration. She nudged Tanya awake. "Dude. Wake up. Class is over." She didn't wait for her and walked out of class. As she left the building, she felt someone grab her arm and stop her.

"Hey! Why'd you leave without me?" Tanya asked, panting.

"Because I'm so sick of this!" Maia exclaimed, stopping in the middle of the entryway.

Tanya cocked her head in confusion. "Okay first, calm down. What are you talking about?" she asked, letting go of Maia's arm.

"This! You!" Maia's voice rose. "You're never paying attention in class, your grades are plummeting- possibly because you never know when we have tests- you don't care about anything anymore, you're always asleep when you're supposed to be listening. And when you realise how much work you have to do, who do you call? Me. And who has to spend the next hour trying to explain integration or Shakespeare or whatever to you? Me. Do you really think I have the time to cater to your every little need because of your inability to stay awake in school? Do you think that you're the only one that's going through something or has a lot to study? Cause here's a little reality check for you. You aren't. So please, for your sake and mine, start caring about your future a little. It'll do you good. Daddy's money isn't going to get you very far."

Tanya looked stunned. "Well," she said stiffly. "I didn't realise you felt that way."

Maia rolled her eyes. "You would if you paid attention."

"Look I don't need this from you okay? I get enough of it at home from my parents and brother and whichever relative is visiting that day. I don't need it or want it from you too. So please, take your opinions and keep them to yourself," Tanya snapped, and began to walk away.

"Oh sure, walk away now," Maia called after her. "But maybe over this weekend, when you're sitting in your room all alone, wallowing in self- pity, you'll start to realise I'm right. And when you do, I'll be here to help you. But until then, my phone will be unavailable for you."

4

Garcia

"No."

Garcia felt his blood boil. Nobody ever said no to him. Nobody had the nerve to. But now, as the man sitting across from him said it, he heard the finality in his voice. Garcia had noted his weak character the first time they met - being partially crippled didn't help his situation- but every time he behaved differently, it got on Garcia's nerves. He didn't need the moral police. He needed someone who could listen, and execute. That was why Garcia had employed Dube in the first place as an assistant. Later, when Dube was reluctant to leave the safe haven of his home country, Garcia decided to put him to use in a different way.

"What do you mean, no?" Garcia reiterated, his hands freezing.

"I think the word means the same in most languages." Dube was clearly enjoying this.

"Look, you can't say no to this. This is your job and mine on the line as well. We have to do this. There is no other option."

"Why can't we think of something else then? Why do we have to do this?"

"Do you have a better plan?"

"How about something that is less *illegal?*"

"To hell with illegal. No one will even get to know! It's a simple give and take," Garcia replied, with rising anger. He didn't need this from Dube right now. He gripped the edges of the table and leaned forward. "Look. The decision-" Garcia spat, "isn't yours to make. You, just need to do as I say. Your job is in my hands. One call, and you are back on the streets, penniless." Garcia thrust his finger in Dube's face in anger, loosening his grip on the table.

"I still can't say yes. It goes against all my principles." Dube said.

"Well then, I guess you'll just have to find a way to change your principles then. And trust me, when I get back, you'll forget what the word even means." Garcia said. Without a glance at Dube, he strode out of the room.

***

Garcia slid the keycard into the slot of his hotel room door. With a satisfying click, the door opened, and Garcia stepped into his room. The bed was still unmade, yesterday's takeout containers still flung open on the study table. He mentally slapped himself for forgetting to take the 'Do Not Disturb' sign off his door. He took his laptop out and typed in his password, and stared at the screen blankly. He had no idea what to do. He had to get Dube on his side in a way that would be credible and creative. He opened up a new document, suddenly set alive with ideas, and began to type furiously. He always got what he wanted. That wasn't about to change anytime soon.

***

Apart from playing with his train set, playing with fire was his favourite thing to do. He was at the corner of the street with his best friend Manny. Their backs were against the wall of an old house, and Anthony had just shown him the matchbox. He had lured Manny to where they were now. He told him he had a new toy, and they would have to be far from home to see it. Manny had excitedly tagged along, eager at the prospect of touching a new toy. Anything new was a rarity for the two of them, as both were younger siblings, and both were poor. At the first sight of the matchbox, Manny flinched away. "Why do you have that? You're not supposed to touch fire! You're too young!" he exclaimed in fright, inching away from it.

Anthony looked at him pointedly. "I haven't even shown you what I'm going to do with it yet," he said, motioning for Manny to sit next to him.

Curiosity getting the better of him yet again, he sat next to Anthony, but a little farther away.

Anthony expertly lit a match, waving it around a scared Manny. He laughed as Manny's lip began to tremble. "Oh quit it! We're nine years old! Act like it! That was just a trial one, come on I want to do something fun." He stood up and went to the front of the house. There was nobody at home, Anthony knew. Not just yet. He had made sure of that earlier. They would be back soon, though, with a lot more people too. "Okay, now it's your turn!" They were next to a clothing line, with clothes crowding the space above them.

Manny looked at Anthony with wide eyes. "Are you absolutely mad?" he said.

"Of course not. Here you go." Anthony lit a match and handed it to Manny with the box, who held it with the tips of his fingers. "Wave it around now, come on, don't be shy," Anthony chided, standing back.

Manny waved the match around slowly, and then faster, under Anthony's watchful and expectant eyes. A small smile slowly appeared on Manny's face.

Anthony took more matchsticks out of the box and handed them to Manny, purposefully ignoring the burning smell that was beginning to surround them.

Manny didn't seem to notice, too preoccupied with his new game. A few minutes later, Anthony looked up at the line of clothes.

"Manny! Look what you did!" Anthony yelled loudly, as the residents of the house came into view.

They gasped in shock as Manny looked up and burst into tears, dropping the matchsticks. "I didn't do it! It was you! You're the one who gave it to me!" Manny yelled, running away from the fire, as the residents of the house poured water over it and hurled insults at Manny. People had gathered around the house to see what was going on. At the sight of Anthony, his mother pushed through the crowd and yelled out his name.

"What are you doing here?" she asked, pulling the both of them away from the commotion.

Anthony feigned tears. "It was Manny, mama. He brought me here and told me he was playing with fire and I told him not to, but he still did and now he's set fire to all the clothes," he sniffled.

Manny glared at him. "I did not! That's not what happened! Stop lying Anthony!" he yelled, bursting into tears.

Anthony's mother pulled him closer. "Oh, my sweet child. Don't go off playing with that monster anymore, you hear me?"

Anthony buried his head in his mother's shoulder. "Don't worry mama, I won't." He turned his head to Manny, gave him a playful smile. "I don't play with people who do bad things."

5

Tanya

Cynical.

Her mother had called her that once. She had known what it meant - *actions done to benefit oneself, without any concern for accepted standards of behaviour-* but she had no clue how it applied to her.

I care what people think. I help others and do things for others. She was twelve then.

Now, at the age of 17 - almost 18, she understood that was exactly what she was. She realised she couldn't care less about other people; she obviously didn't, because then Maia's phone wouldn't be with her, and their friendship wouldn't be on tenterhooks again. Tanya turned around and looked at herself in the mirror. Her dark brown hair was messy. Her uniform was crisp and fresh, something that was unusual for Tanya. She loved her uniform but she never found the time to take care of it. She often found herself wearing the same shirt day after day without washing it. She grabbed her bag, slipped Maia's phone into it, and exited her room, carefully shutting her door behind her and locking it.

She headed to her first class- English, rubbing her arms with her hands; regretting her choice to not bring her jacket along. She walked into her English classroom, and headed towards her usual seat next to Maia, when she saw another girl sitting there.

"Oh and find yourself a new seat in class. The one next to me won't be so inviting anymore."

Anger bubbled inside Tanya, the kind that started a fire inside her chest. She fought the bile threatening to make a show. Ever since her mother's outburst back in Delhi, Tanya found herself unable to control her emotions. Now, as she glared at Shanaya and Maia, she told herself to stop. Subconsciously, she felt her hand reach out to grab the first thing she could find- a mechanical pencil sharpener from the teacher's table- and slipped it into her messenger bag. As soon as she felt her bag get heavier, her head snapped up, and she looked to see whether anyone had seen her. Luckily, everyone had their heads bent over a book, a phone, or was talking to a friend. Save for one person, Maia. She gave her a look mixed with pity and disappointment, and turned to pay attention to what Shanaya was saying. Tanya felt her vision go blurry, and ran to the back of the class to take the farthest seat away from Maia and Shanaya.

On cue, their English teacher walked in. Everyone straightened up and took out their things as the teacher slapped her books down on the table and glared at everyone from over her glasses. "Your assignments are due today. I will call out your name in roll number order, and you will come and place your submission on the table," the teacher said, sitting down and getting the class list from a folder.

Tanya stopped cold. *What assignment?* She immediately went into panic mode, trying to come up with a good excuse for why she hadn't done her work. As students got up and placed their assignments on the table, Tanya felt her stomach twist and turn.

"Tanya Sharma." The teacher said, and looked directly into Tanya's eyes.

"Um...Miss" Tanya began, words tripping over themselves in her head to form one big blob of nothing.

"Ah of course, there's always one. You forgot, didn't you? Come here." The sickly sweetness in her voice send a chill down Tanya's spine.

She dropped her bag on the floor and slowly walked towards the teacher's table. She went and stood before her teacher, who had a sadistic smile on her face.

"You haven't given your earlier assignment either, have you? Or the one before that? How long did you think you could get away with it, hmm? For the rest of the year? I think a visit to the Principal will give you that little bit of inspiration you need."

Tanya's heart fell. She had known that a visit to the principal's had been looming above her for a while now. "Fine," she muttered and headed towards the door.

The teacher looked visibly surprised as she left the room soundlessly, head bowed. Every step she took in the corridor was magnified to ten times its actual sound, each step reminding Tanya of just how alone she was. She stepped out into the morning sun, and leaned against the brick wall of the building. The scorching heat felt good on her back. She heard footsteps behind her, and began to walk faster.

"Tanya, wait!" It was Maia.

Tanya's heart lifted. Was she going to be forgiven? Slowly, she turned around, fighting to keep her smile back.

Maia held Tanya's bag in her hand. "I was sent to give you your bag. And she said I was supposed to make sure you actually went to the Principal's," Maia said flatly.

Tanya's heart sank. She silently took her bag from the other girl and began to walk towards the main building in the middle of the school grounds. Maia went ahead, keeping a safe distance between them. As they approached the front desk, Tanya was hit with a sudden wave of courage.

"I have a valid reason you know. For doing what I did," she murmured, loud enough for Maia to hear.

Maia exchanged a few words with the receptionist and then handed Tanya a slip.

"I'll be waiting here. Make it quick," she said indifferently as though she hadn't heard a word Tanya had just said.

Her eyes fixed to the ground, Tanya took the slip from Maia and turned the knob of the Principal's office. "I know you heard me, don't pretend you didn't," Tanya whispered as she crossed Maia and entered the Principal's office.

The meeting was short and quick, thanks to the fact that Principal Sengupta had a Board meeting to go to. When Tanya left the room, the school bell rang, signalling the end of the first period.

Maia was seated on one of the bright coloured futons and absentmindedly flipping through an old yearbook. When she saw Tanya, she snapped the magazine shut. "My next class is in ten minutes. You have five to explain yourself," she said.

Tanya breathed a sigh of relief. She sat down on the couch opposite to Maia, and framed a crafty story in her head.

6

Mahesh Dube

By the time Dube got home, his body was jittery with anxiety What was Garcia going to do? And more importantly, what was he going to do?

In his younger days, Dube had done several things at the demand of others. Homework, chores, even taken beatings, but this, what Garcia wanted was more than he had bargained for.

His phone buzzed. Garcia had sent him an email. He clicked on it, letting his muscles relax against the wooden bed frame. In the email a smiling young girl stared back at him, her eyes bright and wide, as if she were laughing at a joke. *She can't be more than eighteen*, Dube thought, as he scrolled further down. He was right, she was seventeen. He clutched his phone tighter, his knuckles whitening. He couldn't do it. He couldn't rob a young girl of her life just for Garcia's benefit.

He turned his phone off when his mother knocked on the door. His mother peeped in, her grey hair escaping from its tight bun. "Dinner's ready," she said, a wide smile on her face. When she got a full view of his room, her nose wrinkled in distaste, and she moved to clear off his bed.

"Very bad. Such a dirty room! You're not a young boy anymore!" She scolded, putting his coat on a hanger.

"Leave it Ma, I'll do it later. I'm really hungry," he said, leaving the room.

He hardly noticed what he ate, despite the fact that dinner was one of his favourite parts of the day. He finished quickly and stashed the plate in the sink, bidding his confused mother goodnight. His phone rang. Garcia's name flashed on the screen. Dube's stomach twisted, and the meal he had settled like lead. He put the phone to his ear. "Hello."

"Did you read through my email yet?"

"Yes, I'm still not interested."

"You didn't read the whole thing then?" Dube could almost see Garcia's smirk at the other end. "I'm sure it would change your mind."

Garcia hung up.

Dube opened the email again, and scrolled all the way to the end. As he read the last sentence, his heart skipped a beat.

Head of Operations: Mahesh Dube

He would be head. In charge. His heart raced, as he thought of the consequences. But this wasn't about him. He was still putting a young girl's life in danger. If they were caught, he would surely end up in jail. But if he finally put his brilliant brain to use, how would the police even know? And she was not any girl. Dev Mishra's daughter. That made it personal. And if the plan worked, Garcia would forever be indebted to him. He –Mahesh Dube - would have saved Garcia's company from drowning. He would be a hero, a saviour.

He looked down at his phone again. And read his future title again. And again. And again. The 14th time he read it his mind was made up.

7

Anita

Anita enjoyed clean kills. The messy ones took too much time, and if there was anything Anita didn't have, it was patience. Now, as she slowly extracted the knife from the prostrate body sprawled in front of her, she sighed in exasperation, when she saw the mess she had created.

Man, I really liked this shirt. She stood up and headed to the bathroom, and washed the knife clean of blood. She quickly dried it, and slipped it into her boots. She stepped outside, in search of a mirror. She found one in the corner of the small, rundown apartment she was in. She tilted her head and looked at her shirt from different angles, to see if the blood could be seen. It faintly resembled roses blooming across white canvas, but was still unmistakably blood. In the end, she decided on tucking the shirt in, which fairly covered up all the spots. She pulled her raven hair back from her face and pushed it back into its tight ponytail. She took out her cleaning supplies from a small briefcase and set to work. Half an hour later, she took out her phone, and texted '*Done*' to her client.

A few minutes later, her phone buzzed, a text waiting for her. *Good.* It said. *You will receive your money at the discussed place and 10:30 p.m. today.*

Every time, she received money, a little piece of her heart was joined back together. A little piece of her life was put back together. She slipped her phone back into her pocket, picked up the briefcase and began to make her way out of the apartment. She stepped over the dead body, and turned the knob of the door. As she closed the door, she chuckled. "Good night, sleep tight," she whispered to the dead body, and shut the door tightly.

When she exited the rundown building, the midday sun hit her face and made her eyes burn. It had been an unusually hot December, and Anita hadn't been enjoying it. She pulled her shiny new Ray-Bans from her shirt pocket and had almost put them on, before hurriedly putting it back into her briefcase. She didn't want to stand out. She rubbed her shoes in the sand to make them appear dirtier. She spotted her bike further down the road and began walking towards it.

The neighbourhood she was in was very much like the one she grew up in. Street vendors shouted out their best deals, while buyers bargained for lower prices. Cars swerved through the narrow road, narrowly missing people, who didn't even notice the presence of the car. Her heart fluttered, as she noticed the tiny little details in every person- something she used to do ever since she could remember.

She heard loud male voices shouting behind her, and turned around to see what the matter was. She saw three heavily built men glaring at her, and they were quickly coming her way. Realizing what was happening, Anita slipped into the narrow adjacent street and began to run. She moved as fast as her feet allowed her, navigating her way through the dense crowd of people filling the tiny street. She heard the men behind her catching up, and pushed herself to run faster. The men behind shouted words and broken sentences in a mixture of Kannada and English, threatening her to stop before they took out their guns. She paid no attention to their words, knowing all too well that the 'guns' they spoke of didn't exist, and even if they did, they wouldn't dare shoot in such a large crowd. As she got past the throng of people and reached a little clearing, Anita felt a large hand wrap around her wrist, momentarily stopping her. Instinctively, she turned around and kicked the man straight in the nose with a stellar roundhouse kick. The pointy toe of her shoe hit the man squarely in the face, and he screamed in agony. He staggered backwards and began to run in the opposite direction. The other two men, having stopped in front of her, decided against continuing their futile pursuit and disappeared. Pushing the stray hair away from her face she heaved a sigh of relief. She didn't know who those men were, or where they had come from, but she didn't care. What mattered was she had scared them away before they could ruin anything.

Anita had built her career with extreme vigilance and she couldn't be stopped now. As a child, she had dreamt of having a lot of money and being able to provide for herself and live a comfortable life. And now that she had achieved that, she didn't want anyone, or anything getting in her way. She brushed her pants, getting rid of the dirt that she couldn't see, and began walking towards the main road again. She felt a soft tap on her shoulder. Bracing herself in case it was another goon, she whirled around.

It was a heavily built man in an expensive suit. With greying hair, he seemed to be in his mid-50s. He was not a local, not even an Indian.

"Yes?" Anita asked bluntly, not in the mood for much conversation.

"I saw you back there. With those men. Very impressive." He had a thick foreign accent, his words a strange spiral of syllables.

"Thanks."

"My name is Anthony Garcia. And I'm looking to hire someone." Anita felt sparks of excitement build up in her chest, at the mention of a new job.

"What kind of job is it?" she asked.

"Nothing too complicated, it's just a kidnap."

Anita felt herself deflate. Kidnaps were boring, standard and mundane. Anita didn't do mundane. Kidnaps didn't bring in that much money either.

As if he read her mind, Garcia said: "I'm willing to pay a large sum, and it's not a standard kidnapping."

"How much?"

"Six digits."

"Seven and I'm in."

"Done. Expect a call from one of my men tonight. Your name is Anita Javali right?"

"Yes."

Garcia nodded and walked away. Anita mounted her bike, but not once did it even cross her mind as to how Garcia knew her name.

8

Dube

"Has everything been arranged Dube?"

"Everything's going perfectly according to plan so far. We'll leave at around 10:30 PM, we'll get there by 11. Javali was asked to be there by 11;30 PM," Dube said, closing his office door. He was leaving for the day, when Garcia ambushed him with questions. All he wanted to do was go home for a nice dinner and sleep that was well earned. He had spent the past week scouring through the seedy underbelly of the city, for someone to carry out Garcia's plan. Most sources provided the same name. Anita Javali. A well placed 'walk' for Garcia followed, and their plan had begun to spin into action.

Garcia seemed to have different plans for the evening. He had shown up two hours earlier than he was supposed to, making Dube regret telling him the shortcuts to get to the office quicker. "Seeing as I have nothing to do till then, why don't I come over to your house for a hearty Indian meal?"

Dube felt his soul shrivel in distaste. The last thing he wanted was for Garcia's dark soul to grace his home. He nodded stiffly and turned around, giving Garcia a smile that didn't reach his eyes. "My car's in the basement," he said, indicating that the self-invite had just been confirmed.

***

"Beautiful location," Dube muttered as the two men climbed out of the car a few hours later in front of a large house in an isolated area thirty kilometres out of the main city.

Garcia paid no heed to Dube's comment and reached into the car to pull out a briefcase.

"What's that?" Dube inquired as the two men made their way towards the house.

"Maybe you should stay in the car," Garcia said, looking Dube up and down.

"I'll accompany you." Dube narrowed his eyes and continued to walk.

The house had a purplish glow to it, mist having swathed the whole area like a scarf around someone's neck on a particularly cold night. It was a one-story house with large windows on the top floor. The windows had been broken- probably hit by a stone and all that was left of it were long dangerous shards lining the perimeter of the windows. The windows looked like eyes of a corpse with a lifeless aura. There was a large front porch with a broken 'For Sale' sign stuck to it. At the sight of it, Dube chanted prayers silently in his head, and hoped there was no other-worldly spirit lurking in the house.

Suddenly, the front door opened, and the tall silhouette of a woman, walked confidently towards Garcia and Dube. Garcia quickly moved into the shadows so as to cover his face, and motioned for Dube to do the same.

*

Garcia

Anita Javali looked seasoned to meeting in dark places at the dead hours of the night. She didn't walk, she prowled, her heels muffled against the decaying hardwood floor. Garcia had picked her for a reason. While he could have got a low-quality henchman accustomed to kidnapping, he had wanted someone who knew how to kill. Killers, he had found, were always more careful, and treated their tasks like art, making sure every shade was perfect before touching the canvas.

Anita was like that. He considered himself lucky to have gotten her contact from Dube. But not lucky enough to trust her. He knew she could betray, and she knew he could. He knew how criminals worked. He used to be one. As they shook on their deal, they also secured another. A contract of silence.

*

Anita

At first glance, Anita understood Garcia wasn't to be meddled with. He exuded authority and megalomania. He walked with his hands in his pockets towards her, his Omega watch glinting in the darkness.

"Javali," he said, nodding.

"Give me the cash," she said. She had never believed in small talk, and didn't plan to start now.

He smirked knowingly, as he handed her the briefcase that he held. "That's half of it. You'll get the rest later. There is a file inside too, that has everything you need to know. Your part should be done by no later than 20th December," Garcia said.

As she took it, she realised he wasn't like most of his clients. For starters, she never met her clients, and the people who gave her the money were always scared of her. But Garcia was unconcerned to be around someone with so many shades of crimson staining her hands. He even seemed used to it. She took the briefcase, but not before opening it to glance at its contents.

He wasn't just confident; he was also very, very rich.

9

Anita

Anita was now a lot richer. Her drive home gave her enough time to think. As soon as Garcia left, she had left as well. There was no further need to stay. She got into her car, and opened the file, curiosity running through her body, charging her with a newfound energy. The first thing she saw was the picture of a girl. Her face looked familiar, as though she might have been a relative that Anita had lost touch with, or someone she used to know. Dark brown hair framed her oval face, striking light brown eyes and high cheekbones gave her an ethereal look that Anita couldn't have forgotten even if she tried. But somehow, she had.

Why does her name sound so familiar? She said the name out loud, and her mouth seemed to form the words on its own, as if it were used to saying it. But then why couldn't she remember who it was? She looked through the other pages, most of them talking about where she spent her time, her school, her address. But the main thing missing was the reason for the kidnap. She knew better than to question her clients, but she always found out. There was everything else, every single detail about the girl's life, except why she needed to be kidnapped. Anita didn't put much thought into it, but it was a constant nagging in the back of her mind, reminding her that there was something wrong with this whole project. Or something missing.

✳✳✳

4:45.

Anita had an hour before she had to leave. She rolled out of bed and rushed into the bathroom, only to find the door locked, and the sound of gushing water on the other side of the door.

"Ma! What are you doing in my bathroom?! At four in the morning that too!" She yelled in Kannada in frustration. This wasn't new. Most days, she would wake up to find her mother using her bathroom, when she had her own. The first few times, Anita had said nothing, but lately it had begun to get on her nerves. Her mother would always find one way or another to delay her, and Anita was getting tired of it. She banged on the door again, tapping her foot impatiently.

The door opened, and Anita's mother came out, a large bucket and washcloth in her hand. Her hair was wrapped up in a towel, and she didn't look like she had taken a shower.

"Actually, I was cleaning your bathroom. How was I to know that you would be up so early this morning?" her mother said calmly, walking past Anita and towards the door. Anita felt a sudden wave of compassion for her mother, and began to thank her.

"And besides, I wouldn't want to shower in a dirty bathroom now, would I?" her mother added, and left the room.

They had never been close when she was younger, and things hadn't changed much once she grew up. She had relied on her friends and other elders around her for life advice. She cursed herself for thinking that her mother had wanted to do something other than for herself. Shaking her head, she entered the bathroom, and readied herself for the first day of work for her new client.

***

Anita stepped out of her hut, smiling widely at everyone who passed. Nothing could ruin her day. Birthdays came only once a year and she was determined to remember the time she turned thirteen. She ran down lane after lane of rundown brick houses with asbestos roofs until she reached a bright green door. She knocked on the door, impatiently waiting for it to open. The door opened and her best friend Sachita, stepped out. She was a calm and quiet character, completely opposite to who Anita was.

"Happy birthday!" she said shyly and opened her hand to reveal a small present. It was a bracelet made of soda tabs and held together by small rubber bands of various different colours. Anita gasped and slid it around her bony wrist, admiring it.

"Sachita! I love it! How did you make this all by yourself?" she asked, wondering how long it had taken Sachita to find that many soda tabs.

Sachita blushed and rubbed the length of her arms. "Oh, it was nothing much. I'm glad you like it," she said. "Oh! Before I forget, Umesh also wants to see you. He said he had something for you."

Anita's excitement built again. Umesh was her favourite person. Nobody knew much about him, except that he had committed a heinous crime in his youth. He had been running from the police for ten years, and now had finally settled where Anita used to live. He taught Anita the bread and butter of pick pocketing. Thanking Sachita for the lovely bracelet, she ran again, rushing past people wishing her a happy birthday. Umesh's house was the colour of the bricks. He had never painted it, unlike the other families. She pushed open his door, knowing he wouldn't mind. He was sitting on his rocking chair. He looked up when he saw her.

"Anita! Happy birthday!" he said, his loud voice filling his tiny house. He reached out behind him, and put an object in her hands. It was a tiny horse, with intricate detailing. "A horse, for freedom and power. The two things I hope you have in abundance as a young woman."

"You made this?" Anita asked, stroking the horse's mane.

"It's no big deal. Now run along, I'm sure you've got things to do," he said, and continued rocking on his chair.

Anita gave him a wide smile and ran out of his house, already loving what the rest of the year would bring.

✳✳✳

Leaning against the school wall, Anita tried her best to look natural. At any moment, the students of the large school in front of her would be pouring out. Her eyes were trained on the large front doors. As soon as the large clock struck three, students began rushing out all at once. Several were headed towards the gate, while some milled about inside the school, forming little groups with their friends. Others made their way towards the far end of the school, and disappeared behind the large buildings.

Suddenly Anita realised that she didn't know whether her target went to day school or boarding school. Five minutes later, she saw someone who resembled the girl in the photo. In anticipation, Anita moved closer to the main gate, when she noticed the security guards looking at her closely. She motioned for them to mind their own business with a few suggestive words, and turned her eyes to her next victim. She was walking with another girl, but unlike most friends, they were standing a few paces apart from each other, and seemed trapped in an uncomfortable silence. Her target, then leaned over to say something to the other girl, and in response her face lit up, and she nodded her head vigorously. They both walked a little faster towards the school exit. As they walked through the school gates, the other girl looked at Anita for a second, but her gaze slipped, and moved onto other people around.

Past the gates, both of them turned left, in the opposite direction where most of the children were going. Keeping a good distance between herself and the two girls, Anita began to follow them. They turned into a small café, at the end of the street. It was called *The Hub*, and a lot of the other school students were there as well. Anita was welcomed by the smell of brewing coffee, and another smell which she could only describe as *café*.

The two girls went up to the counter and got their drinks, and grabbed a table by the large window. Anita sat a few tables behind them, inconspicuous.

"In all honesty, do we really need this much homework? Whatever happened to work hard play hard? Remember when all the teachers used to say that to us last year?" her target said as she stirred her drink.

"Maybe they got brainwashed over the summer? Or got abducted by aliens and because of the inter-planet travel stress they lost their memory?" the other girl said thoughtfully.

"Inter-planet travel stress? Is that even a thing? Tanya, I forgot you were kind of funny!" Maia said in between fits of laughter.

The rest of their conversation was filled with mindless chatter, and eventually her target got up to leave. "I should get going. Ramesh will be here any moment, and I have to get home," she said as she picked up her bag and slung it over her shoulder.

"Well, tell him I say hi,' the other girl –Tanya- said, remaining seated.

Maia nodded and chuckled as she left the café.

Anita decided to wait around to find out a little more about the other girl. It was too late now to follow her target back. She knew she was going home anyways, and Anita already knew where that was. Tanya finished the last few sips of her drink. Leaving two ₤10 notes under her empty glass, she left the café. A few minutes later, Anita got up and left as well, but not before slipping the two ₹10 notes into her pocket.

Old habits die hard.

✳✳✳

Anita stood in front of the school gates again, mentally kicking herself. She had lost Tanya in a sea of people, and was unable to find her again. She hoped that Tanya had gone into the school, and would come out again. She asked the security guards whether students were allowed to come out after the main gates closed after dispersal, but the guard gave her a strange look. The thought of having wasted a whole day when there was so much work to do frustrated her.

Ten minutes later, Anita walked away from the school, and towards the nearby mall, where she suspected that Tanya would be. In the midst of the crowd, she felt someone's hand slip into the back pocket of her jeans- the pocket where she kept her wallet. Having been a former pick-pocket herself, she knew exactly what she had to do. In a swift movement, she reached out behind her and grabbed the hand of the pick-pocket. Holding on tightly, she turned around and received a hugely convenient surprise.

It was exactly who she hoped it was. A small smile played on Anita's lips at the sight of the girl's guilty face.

"I'm so, so sorry," the girl said, her eyes widening. She quickly handed Anita her wallet back.

"Oh, that's perfectly fine." Anita replied snidely, her brain working like a well-oiled machine, as several different ideas formed in her head at the same time.

"Can you please let go of my hand? And please, please, don't tell anyone about what happened. Please. Things are bad enough already," she pleaded.

"That depends. How does that work in my favour?" Anita said.

Tanya looked at her for a second, then muttered, resigned. "Fine. What do you need?"

The last piece clicked into Anita's brain, completing the puzzle. "Information. And work."

10

Maia

You have 1 new message.

Maia's phone buzzed next to her on her study table, indicating that she had received a new DM on Twitter. She felt a leap in her heart. She already knew who it was. She smiled as she opened it.

8:45 p.m.

@ayaan_gupta: Sorryyy, I had a lot of homework last night. :((I would have much rather been talking to you though :)x

8:45 p.m.

@mezzomaia: That's no problem :) What're you up to?

8:46 p.m.

@ayaan_gupta: Nothing much, but I heard this song on the radio today and it reminded me of you.

Maia melted. Every bone in her body turned into dust, every muscle into mush. She didn't know what to reply, and continued to stare at the screen, a wide smile playing on her face.

8:48 p.m.

@ayaan_gupta: Heyy where did you go? Oh my God I'm sorry if that was weird for you. I didn't mean to scare you off, come backkkkkk

Involuntarily, Maia began to giggle. She moved her thumbs over the keyboard quickly, mapping out a reply.

8:49 p.m.

@mezzomaia: Haha no, it's okay, what's the song called?

8:49 p.m.

@ayaan_gupta: I don't know the name of it, but it was about a beautiful girl, and that did it for me :)

Her cheeks burned, and she closed her eyes for a second.

8:50 p.m.

@mezzomaia: You think I'm beautiful?

8:50 p.m.

@ayaan_gupta: It'd be a shame not to. You're the most beautiful girl I've seen since-well, ever.

Unable to contain herself anymore, Maia got off her chair and did a little happy dance. She had begun to talk to Ayaan only a few weeks ago, but he had already made her feel special. She walked across the room, to the full-length mirror, and cocked her head to the side. *What does he see in me? Why does he think I'm pretty? Was it her hair?* It was wavy and long, and she'd got it coloured over the summer, but it wasn't that special. *Was it her eyes?* People often complimented her chocolate brown eyes. She made her way to the floor length mirror in her room, and cocked her head to the side. She was thin, that was for sure. Her skin was tan, and her arms were toned, but she had a long, unattractive scar running down her right arm. Maybe it was her profile picture? Maia jumped over to her phone, and realised that she still hadn't replied.

8:55 p.m.

@mezzomaia: That's so sweet! Sorry, but I have to go for dinner :(Talk later?

8:55 p.m.

@ayaan_gupta: I'm right here :)xx

Maia's heart lifted. Giddy with happiness, she put her phone down and decided that the why didn't matter. Somebody thought she was beautiful. Somebody liked her for who she was, and it was a feeling nothing could beat. She ran down the stairs, hearing her mother call her for dinner.

✳✳✳

10:20 p.m.

@mezzomaia: Heyyy I'm backk :)

10:21 p.m.

@ayaan_gupta: You take two hours to eat? xD

10:21 p.m.

@mezzomaia: Nonono I had some school work to finish. I have this essay to do for my senior project, and I have absolutely nooo idea what to do :((I'm really confused.

10:21 p.m.

@ayaan_gupta: Really? What's it about? Maybe I can help?

10:21 p.m.

@mezzomaia: We need to do an essay on any word that holds specific meaning to us. A word that's really special to us.

10:22 p.m.

@ayaan_gupta: Ohhh, that's hard :/

10:22 p.m.

@mezzomaia: I know :(#selfpity T_T

10:23 p.m.

@ayaan_gupta: Hey, did you know the best way to get rid of self pity is to hang out with this really cool and amazing dude named Ayaan tomorrow night at 9:00 p.m. at the Jakkur Airstrip?

10:24 p.m.

@mezzomaia: Are you asking me out? Because I'm pretty sure I saw that very same line on the Internet just a few days ago. Creative;)

10:25 p.m.

@ayaan_gupta: Hey, being original is too mainstream anyways. But would you like to?

10:26 p.m.

@mezzomaia: I would love to :) But isn't Jakkur Airstrip like really empty? And it's government property, therefore- illegal to enter?

10:27 p.m.

@ayaan_gupta: Living life on the edge;) It's usually isolated anyways- and it's going to be empty tomorrow for sure, I did my research.

Maia squirmed in her bed. The idea of doing something unruly excited her, but did she really want to do it? After all these years of leading a restricted life, did she want to break it? She hesitated for a second, and then replied.

10:30 p.m.

@mezzomaia: See you tomorrow then :)

10:30 p.m.

@ayaan_gupta: HA YASSSSSSSSSSS. I mean- Great :-) See you tomorrow :) (Finally, if I may say so)

11:35 p.m.

@mezzomaia: Hey, can I ask you a slightly weird question?

11:36 p.m.

@ayaan_gupta: Shoot

11:37 p.m.

@mezzomaia: What colour are your eyes?

11:37 p.m.

@ayaan_gupta: Brown. Light brown. My friends say they're the colour of hazelnuts.

Tanya

"Tanyaaaa! Get out of the bathroom- we're going to be late! And I need to tell you something important. Like really, really important!" Maia sang from outside Tanya's bathroom.

"I'm done! Just two more minutes!" Tanya yelled back as she deliberately pulled her hair into a messy ponytail. She unlocked the door and stepped out, leaning against the door frame. "Spill."

"Okayyy, so there's this guy," Maia said, a wide grin on her face.

Tanya's heart fluttered, and her grin reflected Maia's. She ran to the bed and jumped on it, and put her hands forward. "I want details. Anything and everything. Don't you even dare leave a single thing out okay?" She half-shrieked, not wanting to be too loud in case people outside heard them.

"Well, it all started - I don't know, maybe two weeks ago? He suddenly friended me, and I friended him back- obviously, I mean, you should take a look at his face-" Maia fanned herself, "but anyways, he liked my profile picture after that, and then DM'd me, and then I DM'd him back, and stuff just zoomed from there. His name's Ayaan, and he goes to the boys boarding school pretty close from here. I don't remember exactly, but I think he's in Pacific. I bet he's like super smart. I heard it's really hard to get in there. And you know the best part? He wants to meet me! Tonight! Like tonight tonight! I'm so excited, I can't even think!"

"Ahhh! What does he look like?" Tanya squealed, excitement bubbling out of her. In that moment, she felt quite pleased with herself.

"One sec, I'll show you," Maia said, whipping out her phone from her pocket. She went into Instagram and gave her phone to Tanya, not realising the oddness of the situation. Phones had become some sort of a taboo between the two of them. "We usually DM each other on Twitter, but I like his Instagram pictures better. There are more of them," Maia said, heat rising up in cheeks.

Tanya gave Maia a small smile and looked down at the phone. He was really good-looking, she couldn't deny that. He had black hair and hazel eyes, and wore beanies. What was not to love? *Good choice.* She scrolled down through the pictures.

"Haha, I know right?" Maia said, laughing.

Tanya's head shot up. "Oh sorry, did I say that out loud? I didn't mean to. I was just thinking out loud I guess."

"Speaking of thinking, class starts in five minutes. We should really get going. I need a *lot* of help. I'll see you during break yeah?" Maia said, picking up her bag.

They left Tanya's room. Maia hobbled a little, still sore from her injury a while ago, but both of them reached the academic building with two minutes to spare. Tanya rushed into the Foreign Language Department as Maia limped into the Math Department, barely in time for the first class of the day.

✳✳✳

"Why don't you stay over tonight? I mean, I can help you get ready and stuff. You need to be prepared," Tanya asked Maia.

"Dude, I'm going on a date, not into war," Maia replied as they stood in the lunch line, balancing their trays in their hands.

Today's special was lasagne and butter *naan*. Nobody in school understood why the two were paired together, but both combinations were popular judging from the size of the lines. Tanya usually opted for the lasagna, while Maia went for the naan and stir-fried vegetables.

"Who knows, maybe you have to," Tanya muttered to herself, hardly loud enough for Maia to hear. "Anyways, you wanna stay?"

"I guess I could, but won't it be hard to sneak out of school?" Maia asked with uncertainty.

"Absolutely not. Its way easier than you'd think. I've done it a bunch of times. Plus, we're pretty much the same size, and I have this really cute dress you could borrow. You left over these killer heels when you came to visit over the summer so I have those in my closet as well." Tanya replied, seating herself at one of the few two-seater tables.

There was chatter around them, most of it focused on Disco Night. "Ew Disco Night," Maia said, puncturing Tanya's lasagna with a fork.

"Ew indeed, and also a perfect getaway," Tanya replied.

Disco Night had started recently, when the students of the school begged for more fun events. The Cultural Committee stumbled upon disco balls, a prop leftover from many plays ago, and Disco Night was created.

"Are they the shoes with the really sharp spikes on them?"

Tanya nodded in reply.

"I've been looking for those everywhere! You hadn't taken them, right? Like on purpose?" Maia asked, a flash of worry crossing her face.

Tanya stopped eating. "Of course not. Why would you think that?" she said icily.

"No reason- I was just making sure. For my sake. I completely trust you," Maia said reassuringly, but Tanya couldn't shake it off.

She shifted in her seat, and continued to eat. "Hey you never told me where you guys are meeting," Tanya said.

"Oh yeah. You know the Jakkur Airstrip? Apparently, Ayaan can 'pull some strings' and get everything set up. And he said it's going to be empty tonight because there was some show or something."

"The Jakkur Airstrip? Does that belong to the government? Isn't that illegal?" Tanya questioned.

Maia shrugged. "He said he had it all figured out. I'm sure my parents won't mind. They're in Switzerland right now, anyways. I guess I'll stay." Maia looked down at her phone. A stupid grin crept over her face, as she stared at it.

"What is it?" Tanya craned her neck to look into Maia's phone

"Ayaan sent me a message while I was in class!" Maia squealed. Tanya squealed back at her and grabbed the phone from Maia.

11:12 a.m.

@ayaan_gupta: Can't wait to finally see you today :) xx

Tanya shrieked again and passed Maia's phone back to her. "You have to look absolutely gorgeous! Not a single hair out of place," Tanya said, as they headed to their last class of the day.

***

"Show me the dress! Show me the dress!" Maia sang as she jumped up and down on Tanya's bed.

As Tanya leaned in to pull it out of her closet, she couldn't help but feel a twinge of guilt. Shaking it away, she took the dress off of its hanger and handed it to Maia.

"It's so beautiful! I never knew you had this!" Maia gushed, stroking the soft lace on the dress.

"Well don't waste your time looking at it, go and actually try it on! You don't have much time y'know," Tanya said, a small smile on her face.

Maia laughed and ran into the bathroom, jumping over the mounds of other clothes she had tried on and discarded. As the bathroom door clicked shut, Tanya fell onto her bed. She stared at the ceiling, gulping nervously. So close. Yet so far away.

Two minutes later, the bathroom door opened, and Maia stepped out. The dress fit her perfectly, stopping mid-thigh. Maia looked beautiful, there was no denying it, but so did every other animal before it went into the slaughterhouse. Maia twirled around in her place. "Well? How do I look then?" she asked, her eyebrows raised.

"Beautiful. You look stunning. The dress fits you perfectly. You're going to have to keep it. I mean, obviously," Tanya replied, plastering the most convincing smile she could muster up on her face.

"So how do you think I should do my hair then? You should do it actually; you're really good at hairstyles. I was thinking I'll leave it open but maybe you could clip it up? I want to show off my new hair you know?" Maia said, posing.

Tanya motioned for Maia to sit down in front of the small dressing table and stood behind her. She expertly did Maia's hair and makeup.

Lastly, she clipped Maia's sparkling diamond bracelet onto her wrist and took a step back to admire her work. "Oh oops, we forgot about the shoes. One second," Tanya said, handing Maia her shoes, careful not to get cut on the large sharp spikes.

They were black platform heels, the heels having large spikes on them, which someone could actually get cut on. The fact that it could be used as a personal weapon is what made Maia buy it in the first place. "Do you really think I should wear these ones? I mean, don't they look like a murder weapon or something? Because I don't want to come off as a murderer. Like obviously. Because that would be kind of creepy. And awkward. An-"

"Maia. Calm down. You're rambling. And who knows? Maybe you'll have to kill someone?" Tanya said, chuckling, her heart dropping into her stomach.

"Oh. Right. Sorry. I'll shut up now. When are we going to leave?" Maia asked nervously, fiddling with the end of her dress.

Tanya checked her phone. It was 8:30 p.m. "Maybe in the next ten minutes? Everyone will be finished with dinner then, so there'll be a huge crowd, and we can go by unnoticed. It's Disco Night too, so everyone will be dressed up. Everything should work out perfectly. Well, hopefully," Tanya added as she got up to look out of the large window.

Downstairs, on the large lawn with illuminated disco balls at the four sides, she saw students dancing to music. Teachers patrolled around the perimeter of the field, making sure nobody decided to do a little 'nature research' behind the bushes.

"Yup, we'll definitely leave unseen. We can walk right through the people. It's just about the timing. We need to make sure there's no teacher around. Because that would be a disaster," Tanya said.

"I have to admit, I'm a little scared with this whole 'sneaking out' business," Maia said.

"Oh, come on! Don't you trust me? Everything will be just fine! You can't stay too long. You might have to, though. We should aim to be back in an hour," Tanya replied.

"What d'you mean - I might have to stay longer?" Maia questioned a quizzical look on her face.

Tanya froze. "Did I say that? Well you know, in case you want to spend some more time with each other."

"You've been really mysterious lately you know?"

I'm being mysterious? Must be because of the recent mystery books I've been reading." Tanya said quickly. Maia rightly decided to leave it alone by then. Tanya stared out of the window. Maia joined her at the window, and as they stared out into the night, Tanya couldn't help but feel nauseous.

✱✱✱

As Bangalore said goodbye to the monsoon and put on its coat for the winter, for Tanya, the days seemed to get longer rather than shorter. She had been in Bangalore for almost a term, and yet nothing seemed different. She still had no friends, still didn't excel in class, and still could not be the daughter her parents wanted to be. Even 1740 kilometres away. As the night fell, the moon rose high in the sky, pushing the sun out of its position to reign over the dark. The lights in her room were off, the only source of light, the ghostly silvery beam of the moon cast on the floor, creating shadows of a life that she could not be a part of. She saw her brother in the shadows, holding another award high in the air. She saw her parents congratulating him, thumping his back as hundreds of people watched, gazing at the teenage boy who had accomplished more than any of them ever would. She saw her memories one after another, and it wasn't long until she realised she was hardly a part of them.

12

Anita

"I don't see the big problem here! It's just a matter of trust! Don't you trust me?!" Anita's mother shouted at a frustrated Anita.

"But why do you need to know? Why does it bother you so much? I'm bringing money into this house! You don't need to work in people's houses anymore, cleaning after them! Why can't you just live with that?" Anita shouted back.

"Because I feel odd! I'm the only mother in this whole place who doesn't know where her daughter works and what she does! It's embarrassing! And you leave at all odd hours, just like now, it's 8:45 at night! Who leaves for work at this hour? It's unnatural and unsafe for a woman to be out at this hour! What if something dangerous happens to you? Why can't you just tell me?"

"Maybe I'm trying to protect you! Maybe you being in the dark is for your own good! And so what if I have to leave late at night? Maybe I'm on the night shift? What's it to you! And I'm getting really late, I have to go. This is a complete waste of time. And every second of time wasted here, is money lost," Anita muttered furiously typing on her phone. She turned around, when she felt a bony hand grab her elbow and swing her around.   "Don't you think it's funny?" Anita said when she faced her mother. "Isn't it funny, how when I was younger you never cared about me? Never bothered to check up on me to see if I was okay when I cried? Never bothered to even take a second glance at me, your very own flesh and blood? You always went away, to your employers' houses, and took care of their children, fed them, even went so far as to *loving* them, all because their parents provided you with money. It was the same with *appa*. You loved him, cared for him, did everything for him, but only while he had that dosa stand, and brought money into the house at the end of each day. As soon as that stopped, as soon as he got too sick to work, you stopped caring. At the time he needed you the most, you decided you didn't need him anymore. So you left him like that. And when he got better, he made the right decision. To leave. I should've left with him you know? I bet you wouldn't have even cared," she hissed, a sudden rage building up inside of her. She was getting late, she knew that- but she had finally begun to say what she had wanted to say for years. She couldn't stop - not even when her mother looked as if she had been slapped in the face.

"Of course, I would've," her mother started, only to be interrupted by Anita again.

"Don't even try. I knew you wouldn't have. Did you even try to stop *appa* before he left? Try to call him back even once as he walked out of the door? You didn't even bother to look up on him, did you? Well I did, and you know where he is now? Phoenix, Arizona. That's in America. And he's happy. He got a good job in a restaurant somewhere and then got accepted into a paid internship program. Now he's head chef of the restaurant. And he has children. Two actually. But that's not the point of this. The point is, that, you loved *appa* when he brought in the money. I didn't bring in any, so you never cared for me. But after he left, and I started to, you suddenly began to notice me. As if though I was never there before and had materialised unexpectedly out of thin air. But you didn't care about my presence either. You just cared about the money. Soon, you stopped working because I was bringing in enough, and you never cared to ask how so much money got into the hands of a filthy, nonsensical sixteen-year-old. So why? After ten years of ignorance why do you suddenly want to know how I make a living? *Why does it matter to you?*"

Anita's mother's face crumpled. "Anita I..."

"I hope you're feeling terrible. I sincerely hope you feel terrible, because terrible is all I felt for a long time," Anita retorted and left the house, slamming the door behind her. She stepped into her car and lit a cigarette.

I finally said it.

✳✳✳

Her hands shook, as she picked up the receiver, and began to dial the number neatly printed at the bottom of the letter. Ever since he had left, Anita and her father had been exchanging letters to keep up with each other. Today, after five years of exchanging letters, he had printed a phone number at the corner of the page, asking Anita to call him when she got it. The number didn't look like a local mobile or landline number, and it was different than any number she had ever seen. She dialled, pressing each number lightly, as if they were going to jump out at her. As the phone rang, she wondered what she was going to say to him. It was always easier to write, because she could write over a couple of days.

"Hello?" A deep voice said on the other side of the phone.

Anita jumped at the unfamiliar voice. "Appa?" she said softly, unable to recognise her own father's voice.

"Anita! You finally called!" he said.

She could imagine the smile on his face. It was hard, speaking to a voice she couldn't remember hearing. When her father had left, he was still recovering, and his voice sounded nothing like it did today. "How are you? Where do you live?" she asked, fidgeting with the phone cord.

Her father hesitated for a second. "Phoenix, Arizona. That's in America," her father replied.

"Yeah, I know where that is. I can't believe you left the country. The continent," she replied angrily, tempted to put the phone down. It had always been her dream to travel the world, and now her father was doing so in her place. Unless he wasn't all by himself. "I bet you're married too. Left us all alone in the dumps to find yourself a rich American lady," she said furiously.

Her father hesitated. In that second, Anita got her answer. "Yes, I remarried. But she's Indian. Her name is Rita. We both worked in the same restaurant. We have two children. I would love for you to visit someday. Meet them."

Anita's heart broke. She looked at her surroundings, the filth and the squalor, and imagined her father in a huge mansion, in the America she knew from the movies. For some reason, even after all this time, she had expected him to come back into their lives. As her father. As her mother's husband.

"I don't think that would work." She hung up, before she could hear her father reply. She crumbled to the floor. She cried her heart out, pushed out every good memory of her father, until they were at the ends of her mind, forming a constellation of souvenirs she wished she had never kept.

13

Maia

"Did I tell you I really like your outfit?" Maia stage whispered as they crouched behind a large bush.

Tanya rolled her eyes. "No, but thanks. Can we focus now?" Tanya muttered, scanning the crowd.

Maia nodded, crouching down even further - or at least as much as her sky-high heels would let her.

"Okay, come on, the coast's clear," Tanya said and began to crawl towards the large fence. Tanya shoved her phone into her pocket and beckoned for Maia to follow her.

What is she doing with her phone now? Maia thought. She felt too giddy with excitement to care. After about two weeks of talking to each other non-stop, they were finally going to meet. *Aren't you getting a little ahead of yourself Maia?* A tiny voice at the back of her head whispered. *What if he isn't what you expect him to be? What if he isn't who he said he was?* A sudden pain shot up through her leg. The pain still hadn't gone. She groaned in pain, and massaged her leg as they crawled. "I should've worn more comfortable shoes. Or at least put a crepe bandage," she said, wincing as she felt every nerve in her foot scream in pain.

At the lack of a response, Maia looked up and realised she couldn't see Tanya anymore. She frantically looked around- careful not to ruin her hair, and whisper-screamed her name.

"I'm here idiot! The other side!"

She heard Tanya, and looked beyond the fence. Tanya had got out, and Maia was still inside. She saw Tanya pointing to something beneath her. Down there, at the end of the fence, there was a tiny rip. At least- it was tiny at some point. Over the years, and over hundreds escaping and entering school through the tiny rip, it had widened and opened up big enough for one person to fit through, but still small enough for someone to miss if they were on patrol. She quickly slipped through, careful not to let her dress rip.

"I can't believe it took you this long to find the godforsaken hole," Tanya muttered as the two of them walked away from the school on the dirt and dust road ahead of them. The airstrip was a five-minute walk away. "Why don't you check if he sent you anything else?" Tanya asked, as a large bus crossed their path, momentarily stopping them.

Maia unlocked her phone, and squealed.

8:43 p.m.

*@ayaan_gupta: Everything's set :) All that's left is the most important part of my evening/night to arrive. :**

"Well, we better get there quick eh? Don't want to waste any time!" Tanya said, and they started walking a little faster- as fast as Maia's heels and her injured ankle would take her.

✶✶✶

"I don't see anything here," Maia said, tugging at her hair.

They had entered the hangar Ayaan had asked them to enter, but there was nothing, just crates and emptiness.

"Are you sure we're in the right hangar?" Tanya asked, looking at her watch.

Maia looked at the time on her own phone. It was 9:30 PM Maia and Tanya had got there at exactly 8:55 PM. They'd been waiting for 35 minutes and nothing had happened.

"She really should've been here right now." Maia heard Tanya mutter under her breath.

Maia snapped her head to the side. "What did you say?" she asked.

"What? Oh, nothing, it was nothing."

Maia shook her head, and walked behind a few crates as if though she expected someone to pop out of one of them with an extravagant dinner arrangement. When there was nothing, she leaned against the wall in hopelessness. "Do you think he stood me up?" she whispered. *Ha. I told you so.* The voice at the back of her head whispered.

Suddenly, she saw the large door open on one end. She walked forward, her heels clicking against the floor. It was him. He was finally here. Maia froze in her tracks.

Her heels weren't the only ones clicking inside the hangar. She looked at Tanya's foot. Tanya was wearing flats. Ayaan hadn't entered the hangar. It was a woman. She grabbed Tanya's hand and hid behind one of the crates.

"What are you doing?!" Tanya asked Maia incredulously, looking at her with wide eyes.

"There's someone else here! A woman!" Maia whispered, her eyes round with fear. She had never been in a situation even remotely as scary as this before.

Tanya rolled her eyes. "Oh, grow up," Tanya said snidely and walked out from behind the gate.

Maia looked after her, her eyes round with fear. *Why is she acting so weird all of a sudden? What's happening?*

Tanya walked up towards the woman, and stopped a few feet in front of the lady. The lady was tall- six foot maybe- with raven black hair that was done up in a long ponytail. She looked vaguely familiar.

"Anita," Tanya said, nodding to her. The lady- Anita, nodded and said something to her in a low voice. Tanya said something back to her, and pointed her thumb where Maia was hiding. Maia started shaking. What was happening?

Tanya took out her phone and quickly typed something.

A few seconds later, Maia's phone buzzed. You have 1 new message. Maia looked at her *phone in surprise. She unlocked it and opened Twitter.*

9:40 p.m.

@ayaan_gupta: Sorry I couldn't make it today darling. I have a proper reason though, don't worry about that. You see, the thing is, I don't exist.

Surprise! You didn't see that one coming, did you? I have to admit, it was hilarious watching you fall for someone who isn't even real. Sorry, but not really.

~T

T.

T for trust.

T for treason.

T for treachery.

T for Tanya.

Maybe this was just some terrible prank. A horrible dream. A nightmare. Maia squeezed her eyes shut, hoping that when she opened them, Ayaan would be there. She opened her eyes, and turned her head to glance at Tanya. They locked gazes, and the smile Tanya gave her could have turned sand dunes into glaciers. Anita approached Maia. Maia froze with fear. She willed herself to move. She strained every muscle in her body to move, but her brain seemed to have stopped working. Tanya moved towards her too. Suddenly, Maia felt her legs again, and began to run. But her ankle still hurt, and her heels were too high. She hobbled towards the opposite gate as fast as she could.

"There's no use running. We've got you now!" Anita said in a singsong voice.

Maia's blood ran cold. Her brain didn't seem to be functioning, it only screamed run! repeatedly. But she lost her footing. She felt the earth come out from under her, and fell to the floor, falling on the same foot. She screamed in agony, holding her foot. Two strong arms grabbed her own from behind, and she felt the world slipping away from her.

14

Tanya

The guilt was crushing her. Crushing her into oblivion. She sat on her bed, the evening after *that* day. The evening after she had done the stupidest and most selfish thing she could ever have done. She had risked her best friend's, her *only* friend's life, for her own selfish needs. She now sat on her bed, pressing the balls of her hand into her eyes, trying to make everything disappear. The minute she'd slipped away, she realised what she'd done. She ran back to the hangar to see if there was any way she could have possibly saved Maia. She had found nothing- except a single earring. Tanya had given them to Maia last year, and here it was again, in Tanya's hands. A tear rolled down her cheek. The Twitter thing had begun as a joke. A way to get back at Maia after their first fight. For Maia to feel what it was like to trust someone and have them turn their back on you. It had gotten out of control.

After last night, she had remained locked in her room - not bothering to go down for meals- thriving on spare candy and biscuit packets she kept in her room for study hunger. She had skipped class, and feigned being sick. She wouldn't have been able to face the crowd.

Maia's absence at school that day had been understood as just that, playing hooky, until that evening when her driver came to pick her up from school. The teachers went into a frenzy, and the dormitory warden called Tanya to the Principal's office, as the person Maia was seen with last. Tanya trudged down the long hallway of the administrative building, and knocked on the door hesitantly.

"Come in," the Principal said, as Tanya pushed the door open. The room was full. The Principal sat at her desk, while the vice principal, senior mistress, and a host of other teachers along with Maia's driver sat at the conference table.

Tanya gulped nervously.

"Tanya. Please sit," Principal Sengupta said, motioning towards a chair.

"I'm good standing actually," Tanya replied, pulling on the corner of her shirt nervously.

"Very well. Do you know why you're here Tanya?" The Principal's eyes pierced into Tanya's.

"No," Tanya replied hesitantly.

"I understand Maia was with you last night?"

"Yes Ma'am."

"And you were together the entire night?"

"Yes Ma'am."

"On school premises?"

"Y-Yes." Tanya's head began to spin.

"What happened in the morning? Was she still with you?" The Principal leaned forward.

Tanya's heart was racing. What was she supposed to tell them? The truth was too dangerous both for her and Maia. She didn't even know the whole truth herself. She hadn't even had the time to come up with a lie. What if the police found out? Did Maia's parents know already? "No Ma'am. But I think I might know what happened." As soon as she said it, she mentally kicked herself. What was she going to say now?

"What happened? I hope you understand that this is a very serious situation Tanya. Maia's parents have been notified and will be back on the earliest flight."

"We were up late," Tanya started. "She was talking about how she felt so restricted, as if her every move was predictable and how she had no freedom. She said she wanted to break free. She wanted to explore the world and find herself. I thought she was just joking around. But in the morning, she was gone."

"Why didn't you notify anyone about her disappearance? Do you understand the gravity of this situation? She could be anywhere right now! She could be in danger! Her parents could sue the school!" The Principal's voice echoed around the large room, and Tanya cowered back in fear.

"I was sick in the morning. I woke up late and I assumed she went to class! I knew nothing about her disappearance until now! I didn't think she would actually run away!"

The Principal massaged her temple with her hand. "That will be all Tanya. You may leave."

Tanya didn't have to be told twice. She ran out of the office and sprinted all the way back to her room. She opened her closet, and a large laundry bag fell out of it. She choked back a sob and kicked it away. It was like the world was pitting against her, making sure that everything she did had some sort of link to what she had done. She went into the bathroom and turned on the tap. She put her hand under the water and imagined as though the water was coursing through her veins, cleansing her soul, turning her wrong deeds into right. Within a minute, Tanya's eyes mirrored the taps, and she clenched her fist, salt mixing with fresh.

No. You have to stop. This isn't going to help at all. It does nothing to help her. Do something. Anything.

She splashed her face a few times, and turned the tap off. She quickly changed out of her clothes and put on fresh ones. She left her room, grabbing her bicycle keys and a little plastic bag from an inside drawer before closing her door. She slipped the bag into her pocket and took a deep breath.

She had to find Anita.

As she left, Tanya kept her head down, muttering to herself. Many tried to strike a conversation, but she didn't even notice. She ran down the stairs and left the building, the cool Bangalore air hitting her face, the fresh air rejuvenating her. Momentarily. She blew the dust away from her cycle seat and sat on it, testing the brakes and the pedals before starting to move. She upped her speed until she could go no faster, and everything around her was a blur- out of focus, just how she needed it to be. She raced around the school a few times, before slowing down a little, heaving. She pedalled slowly, looking at the buildings. They nodded at each other, and Tanya sped on towards the gates. As soon as she left the school, the warm blood rushing through Tanya's nerves froze. She screeched to a halt, black marks shooting out on the road.

What's she doing here?

✳✳✳

Tanya scoffed. "You really didn't have to check up on me for that you know. Who'd you think I would tell?"

"You can't really trust anyone you know. Especially not someone like you. Do the parents know yet?" Anita asked, narrowing her eyes at Tanya.

They were leaning against Anita's car, Tanya's bicycle against the hood. At the sight of her, Tanya had cautiously cycled her way out of the school. Anita had been standing exactly where she was now, large sunglasses covering her eyes.

"Of course, they know. They're on their way back. I don't think the school is calling the police just yet though." Tanya bit her lip. "I told them she ran away."

Anita cocked an eyebrow. "Hmm. So, you're not entirely useless."

"What happened after I left?" Tanya asked.

"Left what?" Anita replied nonchalantly.

"Oh, don't play dumb. You know exactly what I'm talking about." Tanya replied, turning to face Anita.

Anita smirked. "Why do you care anyway? You're the one who delivered her there, all nice and pretty."

"Just tell me."

"Oh, the usual. I knocked her out, hauled her into the car and chucked her-"

"Please don't use words like that while talking about a human being."

"Will you please let me finish? I chu-sorry, put her into the car and took her to where I was supposed to."

"And where would that be?"

"You don't need to know."

"And why's that?"

"One, I owe you nothing, and two, client confidentiality," Anita said coolly, taking out a cigarette from her pocket.

"To hell with client confidentiality. I need to know where she is!" Tanya whisper-yelled, not wanting to attract any attention, but still wanting to get her anger across.

"No, you don't. What exactly is happening here? Are you suddenly developing a conscience? Well guess what honey, you should've had this development a long time ago, because it isn't going to do anything for you now. You made an agreement, so did I. You have to hold up to your end of it, as do I."

"Wait a second - whose car was it?"

"You're especially nosy, aren't you? I've said this once already, but I'll say it again you don't need to know."

"Well then, I think we're done here." Tanya said.

"I thought the same." Anita said and unlocked her car. She drove away, Tanya's bicycle falling to the road with a clutter.

Tanya huffed, and picked it up. She waited until Anita was a good distance away, and began to pedal behind her as fast as her legs would allow her to.

15

Maia

"Don't you trust me? Don't you trust me baby? Darling, you know I love you. You know you're the only thought that runs through my mind all the time.

You're the one.

The only."

"Don't you believe me? Don't you love me back? Honey, why're you running away? You know I'll be wherever you are. I'll go wherever you go. My heart follows you every step of the way. And besides, where do you even need to be, when everything you want and need is right in front of you?"

He looked exactly as she thought he would. Light brown eyes, the colour of hazelnuts. Dark black hair, sticking up at odd ends, as if someone had run their hands through it. She ached to push them down. He wore a crisp black tuxedo, his bowtie left undone around his neck. His cheekbones were arched, with and his beauty drained the world of all its colour. There was him, and only him- the lone shining sun in a sea of desolation. His face like an ocean before a storm - gentle, harmless and deceiving.

But she saw right through it.

Right through the thin wall.

She began to run, trying to get away from him, from his feigned words. But no matter how hard and fast she tried to move her legs, she remained rooted in the same spot.

He slowly walked towards her, until they were eye to eye. "Darling, there's no use. You're mine. I'm yours."

"Bu-but, you don't even exist! You're nothing! You're just a bunch of lies!" she said, hot tears streaming down her face.

"I may not exist in the real world, but you know you want me to exist. I exist, I do. In your head-" he tapped on her forehead lightly, "- I live. Thrive in fact. I feed on your fears - on your insecurities, until I become them. I'm your very own personal devil. And don't worry, the throne in hell next to mine, is yours. Always," he said, lounging on a large recliner she hadn't noticed before.

"You want one too, pumpkin?" he said, snapping his fingers. Another recliner appeared. He motioned towards it."Sit. Let's have a chat," he said, giving her a smile.

"No. No, I have to get out of here! Let me go!" she cried.

"No! You can't leave! Don't you see? This way, we can be together forever! Just like you wanted," he said, the last part with a sly smile.

She tried to untangle her legs.

"Oh, please. Don't pretend like you hadn't already thought of our children's names. Tell me, did I make you feel rebellious?" He moved close to her. "Make you feel wanted? Maybe even loved?"

She held back a sob.

"I think you need a little something to truly persuade you. Wait a second. I'll be back. Love you," he said with a wink, and disappeared behind a large door.

With him gone, she took a good look around the place. She was exactly where she was supposed to meet him, at the hangar. It was not as well-lit now, the flickering lights cast large dancing shadows on the high walls. They all seemed to be reaching out to her, trying to grab her, diffuse her into the shadows, make her their own. She wriggled her legs again, but they were glued to the ground even tighter now. She wiped her tears with the back of her hand, frustrated at herself.

There was a sound of a door opening, and he returned. But this time, he had someone with him. Someone, who until this day, she thought she knew best. It was her 'best friend'. She recoiled, her body coursing with an emotion she couldn't recognise.

"No. Not her. Anyone but her. Please," she whispered, suddenly losing the energy and urge to fight back.

"Why? Does she pose a threat to you? And look, she's even brought us a gift to commemorate the start of our relationship. Isn't that just wonderful?" he said, smiling. "Come on, why don't you show us what you've brought us?"

"Oh, it would be my pleasure. After all, I picked it out myself," her 'best friend' said, the smile on her face wicked and icy. The 'best friend' opened the box, the smile not leaving her face.

He gasped at the sight of it. Oh my! You've really outdone yourself this time. And you know the best part? I know exactly what I have to do with it!" he said gleefully, clapping his hands like a child.

She itched with the urge to know what was inside, but that would be cooperation. So she held back, looking straight into his gleaming eyes as he put his hand into the box. He took it out, a sharp light bouncing around the room.

A dagger.

Vintage, and it probably wasn't capable of killing anybody; but it looked lethal and frightened her all the same. She held her breath. She knew exactly how it was going to be used.

"Isn't it just beautiful babe? Just imagine the things we could do with it! Would you like to touch it? Hold it in your little hands?" Both of them, him and the 'best friend' began to laugh, the laughter quickly turning into chortling. Their bodies shook, shaking with helpless mirth. Their laughter soon began to die out, but their bodies continued to convulse. They moved towards each other, the shaking of their bodies so fast she couldn't focus on either of them. There was a sudden bright light, and the two bodies crashed, bursting into flames.

She suddenly felt her legs liberate themselves. She backed away in horror. She had to find an exit. She needed to get out of there. This wasn't real.

"Where are you going, my sweet?" the new thing said, the voice a mixture of both the best friend's and his. Their brains had become one, their hands the same, but the face still his.

"What are you? What is all of this?" she whispered, still backing away.

The new creature followed along, dagger raised in the air, eyes a mixture of crazed desire and laughter.

She suddenly heard a thud, and felt her back hit the wall. No. No, this can't be happening, she thought. Please, don't let this happen.

It kept moving towards her, until they were so close their foreheads touched. "This way, we'll always be together," he whispered into her ear, and the dagger came crashing down.

Maia struggled to open her eyes. She felt an invisible weight crashing into her chest.

I mean, you need to be prepared.

And who knows? Maybe you'll have to kill someone?

She struggled, trying to fight the darkness.

Don't you trust me?

Don't you trust me?

The same four words resonated inside Maia's head, several little figures appearing in front of her closed eyes. They said the same words, over and over, until only one remained.

I swear I've changed.

✳✳✳

"Budapest."

"Vienna."

"Vienna? I don't think I've heard that one," Tanya said.

They were sprawled on Maia's king size bed, Tanya on her back and Maia with a notebook in front of her. They were adding to their Epic Trip Of A Lifetime list, a concept curated by both of them when they had first met. After they had finished school, both of them planned to travel the world. Except, they would only go to cities that had their names in a song title. Since the plan had been made, they had become a lot more picky about their choices, trying to put in songs that had only the name of the place as a title or a song that both of them knew all the lyrics to.

"Oh my God! How have you not heard it! It plays in practically every café on this planet!" Maia said. "I'll make you listen to it when I get up; my phone is plugged into my speakers and those are too far away," she said, writing Vienna on her list.

Tanya laughed, used to her laziness. "Okay, what else?" she asked, thinking. "Oh! Berlin!" she said.

Maia nodded in agreement, writing it down.

"Paris."

"*New York.*"

"*Bombay too, but I really think we can skip over that one. I think we've been enough times,*" *Tanya said.*

"*Definitely. How about London? There has to be one with London.*"

"*Oh, London Bridge is Falling Down, obviously. Are we going to completely ignore the fact that you used to live there and you only look for excuses to go back?*" *Tanya smirked.*

"*Yes, that is precisely what we are going to do*" *Maia said with a straight face.*

"*Chicago, write that down.*"

"*Calgary.*"

"*Galway.*"

"*Barcelona*"

"*Tokyo.*"

"*Ibiza.*"

"*Rio.*"

"*Rome.*"

"*San Francisco.*"

"*Do you really believe we're actually going through with this? Do you think this is actually possible?*" *Maia asked, closing the book and turning around to stare at the ceiling.*

"*Of course, we're going to. The only obstacle is that we haven't asked our parents. Mine won't care, yours will need a little persuasion. Maybe if you promise to expand the business,*" *Tanya said, and threw a pillow at Maia.*

"*Hey!*" *Maia laughed and threw it back at her. "Just imagine us, roaming down the streets of Salzburg, singing like the Von Trapp family. We'll go to cafes and listen to men in lederhosen playing the piano while eating strudels.*"

"*I hope you know we're going in the 21st century, not the 20th,*" *Tanya said as she threw the pillow back at Maia. "But there's no chance we're doing all of those things!"*

"Why not?!" Maia asked.

"Because do you want to be a living breathing tourist stereotype?"

"Good point," Maia said.

They continued like this, throwing the pillow back and forth as they came up with plans on what they would do in every city. Anyone who looked in on them at that moment could've sworn that their friendship was golden, and their conversation would stay like this even when they were grey and old. That's what Maia had believed anyway.

16

Tanya

When Tanya could not drill the answers she needed out of Anita, she knew she needed a Plan B. She found it a few minutes later, hidden deep inside her brain- based on a distant memory.

As soon, as Anita left with her car, Tanya followed her. Dust and sand flew behind her as she raced on her cycle to keep up with the car.

When she'd been in the seventh grade, she and her friends had decided to find out everyone's final results before anyone else. Having money to spare, Tanya had gone out the very same day to buy a tiny camera from a spy store. The next day, during the lunch break, Tanya and her two friends snuck into the teacher's lounge. They'd placed the camera on top of the large refrigerator, which had an excellent view of the room. Over the course of the next few days, all the live footage transferred to Tanya's laptop. After their stunt, all the footage had been deleted, and no one had found out. Tanya retrieved camera later, and had kept it, for old time's sake.

When she'd found it again in her dorm room a few months ago, she had kept it safely hidden, in case she needed it again.

And need it she did.

Anita's car drove through the narrowest roads, took several sharp turns, and finally emerged on a main road.

Tanya maintained a safe distance again. A few minutes later, the car turned into a small lane and a few kilometres later, a large house appeared, made mostly of glass and metal. Tanya pulled to the side of the road and admired the house for a second.

It was contemporary with rectangles and squares, and there was hardly any concrete visible.

Stop staring. You came here to do something. Do it, and leave. She chained her bike to a flickering lamp post. Dusk was creeping in, and Tanya had to get back. She tiptoed to the side of the house, and was beneath a large window. The windows were expansive sheets of glass and the lack of curtains helped Tanya see what was going on inside the room. Anita was inside pacing in deep contemplation. The room was sparsely decorated and had an antiseptic vibe to it. Tanya heard a faint noise coming from inside the house. Anita's face twisted in annoyance. She glared and stormed out of the room.

Tanya seized the opportunity, and put her hands on the windowsill. She attempted to swing her legs up, like she'd seen in several different movies, but nothing happened. After four attempts, Tanya successfully hoisted one leg onto the windowsill. Mustering up all her strength, she lifted the other leg up, and lay down on the windowsill for a second, basking in her own glory. Realizing that Anita could return any minute, she got on her knees and slipped her hand through the thin slit of the only open window. With her other hand, she took the camera out of her pocket and placed it inside the room. With a smile, she turned it on, and saw the satisfying red light blink once before it dimmed. The camera had been made perfectly- so small that from far away, you couldn't even see it. In the distance, she heard footsteps, and realised Anita was coming back. She jumped off the windowsill and ran away from the house to her bike, a huge grin on her face.

Her job was done.

For now.

17

Anita

For the first time, the money brought her no joy.

Something didn't feel right. Her work was done, she had received her money, but Anita was still missing something. All she could see was Maia's face, her eyes wide and scared, arms and legs trembling. When she began to run away, it had been too late. Maia had known she was doomed just as much as Anita had known it. But still, Anita had followed. She'd followed Maia and did exactly what she had to do. If it had been anyone else, the whole process would have been like an exciting game of Snakes and Ladders to her.

Anita shut her laptop and walked towards her large dresser, and pulled open a drawer. Piles of lipstick containers and old compact mirrors and brushes littered the surface. She slowly moved them away, creating a small empty space in the drawer. She pushed on it, making the thin white wood bend, until it gave away, neatly falling into the little compartment it had just opened up. Inside the compartment was a small remote, with only two buttons on it. One said ouvrir, and the other said fermer.

Anita had the remote specially designed in such a way that the buttons were labelled in a foreign language. Although French was quite common, her mother didn't understand it, and that was the purpose.

Anita pulled down the blinds, and locked her room door to avoid any visitors or a specific visitor. Aiming the remote at the ceiling, she pressed ouvrir.

The ceiling split into two, revealing a thick wooden panel. With a slight creak, the panel descended closer and closer to the floor, revealing a shiny bookcase made of polished red cedar wood.

It hit the carpeted floor with a slight thud. Several files dating back to 2013 were kept there, each with a single Sticky Note in front, which stated the specific date and the name of the person who hired her. She'd kept every single file, from every single case she'd ever taken, in case the police ever tried to convict her.

The newest file was made of brown leather, and was the thinnest.

She'd been through the information several times in the past few days, but had not found anything useful. She flipped to the end, where an envelope was placed inside the transparent slip. It contained a host of pictures, all of Maia, at different locations with different people. Several had been taken from Maia's social media accounts, but there were others as well- yearbook photos, and pictures from family photoshoots.

Why do her parents look familiar?

She took a deep breath and took out one of the family photos. There was only one person she could ask.

***

"*Amma,* I need to ask you a question."

Her mother's face lit up with happiness, at being spoken to. Anita hadn't spoken to her since the night she had yelled at her. "Yes, yes tell me!" she said, her Kannada nearly tripping over itself. Anita held out the picture to her.

"Who's this?" she asked, motioning for her mother to hold the picture in her hands.

A flicker of recognition passed through her mother's face, and her face broke into a large smile. "You don't recognise them? My, she's grown up so much! I'm surprised you don't remember. You used to beg me to take you with me whenever I went to clean their house!"

"I did? Who are they?"

"The Mishra family! They came from London remember! The little girl- she had the cutest English. No one except her parents could understand what she said," her mother said fondly, her hand on her heart.

***

She entered behind her mother, shy and timid, her hands folded neatly behind her back. Her mother had asked her to come with her that day, saying that her employer's young daughter needed someone to play with.

She didn't want to come, didn't want to do something again to make her mother's employer happy, but she knew she had no choice. Her mother had neatly oiled and pulled her hair into two braids, securing them with a ribbon. She was even allowed to wear her best blouse and skirt.

As soon as the door opened, her mouth fell open. The woman was dressed, in what her mother called 'rich people clothes', and the house behind her, was incredible. Anita put her hands together in front of her, and said 'namaste'. The woman's face broke into a wide grin, and she took her hand. The woman said a few words to her mother in Hindi, and then kneeled down to her level. "What's your name?" the woman asked in crisp English.

"My name is Anita, ma'am" she replied shyly.

"Hi Anita, I'm Vineeta. Please don't call me ma'am! How old are you?"

"10."

"Wow! Double digits! I'd like to thank you for coming over today. I was hoping you could play with my daughter while your mother worked? My daughter is five, but she's a right storm," Vineeta said sweetly.

"Okay."

Vineeta took Anita through the house, and up the big staircase. They walked past door after door, all white, until they reached the last one. The door was baby pink in colour, and had a picture of a crown on it that said 'Princess Maia' on it. She pushed the door open, to reveal a room so large that Anita's whole house could have fit into it. Anita looked around in awe. It was every little girl's dream bedroom. There was a large dollhouse, one that you could walk into, and an identical miniature version of it right in front.

"Maia, baby, look who came to play!" Vineeta said, motioning for the little girl to come over. She was the most beautiful girl Anita had ever seen, with long hair and large chocolate-coloured eyes.

"Who's this, Mum?" the little girl asked inquisitively.

Anita struggled to understand what she was saying. The girl didn't sound Indian at all.

"This is Anita. She's here to play with you so you don't feel lonely," Vineeta said, pushing Maia's hair away from her face. She gave her daughter a smile so bright and loving, Anita felt a pang in her heart. Why didn't she ever get smiles like that from her mother?

"Really? Thank you, Mum!" Maia said, giving her mother a wet kiss on the cheek. She then looked at Anita, and gave her a warm smile. She grabbed Anita's hand and pulled her into the room. "Hi Annie!" she said.

"It's Anita, not Annie," Anita replied with a small smile.

"Oh well," Maia said, and ran into her room.

That day, just as Anita was about to leave, Maia ran up to her.

"I like you," she said decisively.

Anita felt her heart open. "I like you too," she said smiling, and both of them began to laugh.

✳✳✳

Two years. She'd spent every weekend for two years with Maia, and yet she didn't recognise her. She still couldn't remember much, but what she did was enough. Maia had been like her little sister. Maia had made her feel like she had someone who loved her.

How could I have forgotten?

Now, she remembered gushing at Maia's expensive playthings in comparison to her ragged ones. She remembered endless games, and whispered jokes.

Anita suddenly felt the same pang in her heart. The same pang she had felt thirteen years ago the first time she'd met Maia. Love. And Anita wouldn't let anyone she loved walk straight into the hands of death.

Even if she didn't know them anymore.

18

Maia

Maia's 13th birthday was supposed to be a blast. She had organised a party to remember, had the house decorated with state of the art decorations. Her parents hired the best caterers in town. Everything was supposed to be perfect. Except for the fact that her parents were not there. Whisked away on another 'extremely important business trip', she found herself alone on her birthday, yet again.

She woke up to a pile of presents, decorated around her room. She jumped out of bed, ripping them open in an excited flurry. Bits and pieces of wrapping paper flew around the room as Maia marvelled at the presents. Every year, the number of her parents gave her was the same as her age. "One for every year you've lived," they said. This year though, there were only twelve. Having opened them all, she scanned the room again, not out of greed, but because she knew that her parents - no matter where they were, would not disregard tradition.

Her housekeeper came in five minutes later, wheeling in a tray filled with a vast assortment of breakfast foods, all Maia's favourites. As she tucked into maple French toast, her phone buzzed.

Her parents were video calling her. "Happy birthday!" they said, their smiles filling up her screen. "You've probably been missing that 13th gift."

Maia nodded.

"You'll get that soon. It's a surprise!" Her mother beamed at her. Maia's heart lifted for a second.

"Are you guys coming home?" she asked hopefully.

Her father shook his head. "I'm sorry, honey. The earliest we can come is next week. We're really sorry."

"No problem," she said, faking a smile.

✷✷✷

Maia was surrounded by her friends, and was wearing her new dress. Everyone gathered round as her housekeeper lit thirteen candles, and Maia picked up the knife to cut the cake.

The doorbell rang.

"Ah! Your 13th present! I'll get it!" her housekeeper said, and ran to open the door.

Maia waited for her to come back, her heart racing.

Her housekeeper returned, and Maia craned her neck to see what was in her hands. The gift she saw though, was a million times better.

Her parents stood behind her housekeeper, tall and proud.

She screamed and ran towards them, engulfing them in a hug. "Ah! I knew it, I knew it, I knew it! I knew you wouldn't miss my birthday!" she said, holding them tighter, not wanting to let go.

"The thirteenth gift was a shocker eh?" her father chuckled, ruffling her hair.

"You bet," she said, smiling.

✳✳✳

She opened her eyes, expecting the calm hues of her bedroom walls. She stared at the dirty white walls, with dark black handprints and long stains. She sat up with a start, trembling. She pushed away the ragged blanket covering her and put her feet on the floor. She stood up unsteadily, and sank back down, grimacing. She looked down at her foot, and saw a dark purple bruise blooming on her ankle. Gingerly, she removed her shoes, and set them aside. She was in a place she recognised. An industrial shed.

Her father owned several, but none were as big or empty as this. This one was probably the size of a half a football field, and was poorly lit. A chill ran down her spine, as fear started to set in. Her hands felt clammy, and were shaking uncontrollably. She closed her eyes.

You can't be scared. You need to figure this out. You need to find out what happened.

She looked at her hand to see the time, but had no watch. How long had she been asleep? She stood up with caution and limped over to the only window that hadn't been boarded up. It was dawn, the sunrise sending feeble rays of light into the room through the grimy glass. There was a large gate at one corner of the shed, and Maia had little hope of it being open. Next to the door, she saw a small steel plate and a bottle of water.

Her stomach growled in response, and Maia hobbled over to it. She bent down and picked it up. She gulped down the water without a break, even though common sense told her she should ration her supplies. The plate contained only four pieces of dry bread, which she ate without saving any.

When she moved back to the bed, questions flooded her mind. She didn't remember much, just the school day with Tanya, then getting ready later to get ready for her night out with.

Ayaan.

Maia dug the balls of her palms into her eyes, until phosphenes waltzed around her eyes.

No crying. Do. Not. Cry.

Ayaan.

The first time she felt like she was falling in love. It had all been a stunt. Every word, every sentence, a lie.

Tanya? What have I ever done to her? She had kept Tanya's secrets, been there for her when she needed her. And all for what?

The tears finally spilled over and she sobbed in memory of the betrayal. Tanya had dropped hints- so many hints, but Maia had failed to pick them up.

She was still in the same dress she had been in, although one earring and her phone were missing. As morning turned to midday and the shed began to heat up, sweat trickled down her forehead. But she remained where she was- her eyes fixated on the same spot on the floor, too empty to feel anything.

The large gate creaked open, the silhouette of a stout man casting a long, forlorn shadow inside the shed. Maia moved her eyes towards the door, but immediately moved them back to the spot on the floor.

The man pulled a chair and sat down in front of her. "Hello," he said.

Maia didn't even flinch.

"My name is Mahesh."

Maia did not raise her eyes.

"I'd just like to ask you a few questions."

Maia's brain started to whir. She had been trained for situations like these since she was six years old.

"What do you like to do in your free time?" he asked in a friendly tone.

"What's it to you?" Maia said.

"Okay, what are some things that you don't like?"

"Probably you," Maia said. She kept her face expressionless. Her eyes were still fixed on the floor. She understood why she was being held captive. *Why hasn't he started asking the real questions yet?*

"Are you close to your parents?"

Bingo. "Again, what's it to you?" she asked, a small smile playing on her face. She quickly wiped it off her face. *He can't know I know.*

"Please don't make this harder than it already is. Now, do you know what your parents do?"

"Yes."

"Would you like to tell me?"

"No."

Mahesh sighed. "Fine then," he said, and hobbled away.

Maia smiled triumphantly. It felt like her first smile in days.

19

Tanya

"She'll come back, you know? Wherever she is, she'll come back. There's nothing you could have done about it."

Tanya looked up at Shanaya. "But there is. I could've done so much."

Shanaya sighed. The students started to put the pieces together. They had no clue about Tanya's involvement, and Tanya planned to keep it that way.

Shanaya stood up and fiddled with her watch. "I have to go out. I have some errands to run. You want anything?" she asked, moving over to the door.

Tanya shook her head.

"Okay Tanya," she said and left.

Tanya's phone buzzed, her ringtone blaring out of the tiny phone speakers. She reached over to it and flipped it over.

It was Maia's mother.

She contemplated her choices, when she heard a voice from the other end of the phone. "Hello? Tanya?"

What? She placed the phone to her ear. "Hi Auntie."

"I, I don't even know what the right question is here," Maia's mother said. Her voice sounded faint, resigned. "The airport here is shut, there's a snowstorm and I don't know when we'll be able to get out. Our company plane is back in Bangalore too. What happened exactly?"

Tanya had no clue what to say. "Have you spoken to the Principal yet, Auntie?"

"I have, Tanya. But I would much rather hear it from you."

"Well," Tanya said in a small voice. "She said she wanted to be free."

"What does that mean?" Maia's mother's voice broke.

"Did you call the police yet?" Tanya's heart was thumping.

"I fear there may be something more to this. If what we think is true is actually true, then the police may make matters worse. This is very unlike Maia."

Tanya gulped. Did they know? How could they? She had been so careful. Had they received a ransom note? "What do you mean, Auntie?"

"Oh, you're too young to be in the middle of this. Don't worry about it. You take care." The phone clicked, as Maia's mother hung up.

Tanya rubbed her face with her hands a few times, and bent over her bed to pick up her laptop. As soon as she unlocked it, the camera footage from Anita's house opened. The blinds had been pulled, but Tanya could still see the whole room through a tiny slit where the blinds ended. She watched in awe, as a bookcase descended from the ceiling. About five minutes later, Anita picked something out of the file and left the room. Tanya fast forwarded until Anita came back into the room. Anita closed the door and leaned against it, her eyes wide open in shock.

What does she know?

20

Garcia

"No results? What do you mean no results? You had one job! One job. Can you not do anything correctly? Remind me again, why did I hire you?" Garcia yelled, pressing his fingers against his throbbing temple. Dube stood in front of him, looking straight back at him, his black eyes piercing.

The blithering idiot.

"Well don't stand there like that! Go do something about it!" he said, lowering his voice.

✱✱✱

"The first trick to making money, is knowing how to spend it," Mr. Dias said.

"Sir, I like the sound of that. I can definitely do that well," Anthony replied with a smirk, as he fingered the 200 reals he had just received.

"The second, is employing the right people to make it for you," Mr. Dias said, as he took the reals back.

"I can definitely do that," Anthony said. "Sir, my mother's money?" he asked innocently.

Mr. Dias raised his eyebrows and handed him the reals. "Make sure it gets to her properly."

Anthony nodded and ran out of the house. He stepped into a small store at the corner of the street. He slapped the money on the counter. "Gun holster. Leather please."

✱✱✱

He had worked too hard to let everything crumble now. No one was going to get in his way. He would have what he deserved.

"And what do you think I should do?" Dube questioned, leaning against the wall, his arms folded across his chest.

"Now is not the time to be stubborn with me. Remember, it's not for a personal outcome. This affects you just as much as it does me," Garcia said, placing his hands on the table. "Tell me the time."

"11:45 AM." Dube replied, glancing at his watch.

"Date."

"Why?" Dube asked.

"Date."

Dube rolled his eyes. "22nd December."

"Wasn't she brought in on the 20th? Why did you only go today?"

"She was down for two days. Nothing could wake her up."

Garcia swore colourfully. "Do you see how much time we're wasting here? Every minute counts Dube, every minute! Time is money. Hasn't anyone ever told you that? Every second that we put to waste, we're losing more and more money," Garcia said, his voice rising. He stood up and moved towards the door.

"You're useless. I'll just do it myself," he said and stormed out of the room, leaving a relieved Dube in his wake.

***

As soon as his car dropped him in front of the shed, he shoved the door open. He stopped for a second after entering, regarding the largeness of the shed.

Well at least he did something right.

She was sitting on the ragged straw bed, her back against the wall, staring at the ceiling. She did not seem to notice his entry, but that didn't bother him.

"Look, the other man May not have gotten got anything out of you, but I certainly will."

No response.

"I would like you to know that the longer you take to reply, the longer your parents have to suffer."

A flicker of doubt flashed across her face.

Works like a charm.

"You have my parents," she said gruffly. It wasn't much of a question, more of a statement.

"That's right. Now, if you don't tell me exactly what I want to know, things will only go from bad to worse."

"I don't know anything," she said, her eyes returning to the ceiling.

"Ooh, now, if there's something that I don't like, it's a lie."

"You can't get anything out of me. There is nothing to get out."

"Now, tell me everything you know."

"About what?"

Garcia's temper was rising. "About your parents obviously. The company. It's clients maybe."

"I told you, I know nothing." Her temper was rising as well, Garcia could tell.

"Don't lie."

"I'm not lying!" she yelled, standing up unsteadily. She had an angry bruise on her ankle. Her face was reddening, and her eyes were shining.

"How can you prove that?"

"Who are you, anyways? Why am I here?" she yelled, her voice getting louder with every word, tears freely streaming down her face.

"Just answer my question."

"But I don't know! Why don't you understand? They haven't told me anything! I know nothing!" She wailed and sat down on her bed and covered her face with her hands.

With a sound of disgust, Garcia stood up and walked away. Waste of time.

✱✱✱

Anthony crawled underneath the large dining table, his pocket knife gleaming in his small hands. It had been his birthday gift this year from his parents, to protect him from all the evil. Everyone was upstairs, enjoying a board game. He stroked the leg of one table, the one that had been loose for as long as Anthony could remember. It was kept at a certain angle, supporting the table without being stuck to it. Just a little push, he thought. He gave it a little shove, and he heard the table creak. He took his knife and made a little sign on the bottom of the leg - an AG. Much later, in life, although his pride would continue to grow with his evil side, he would also learn the art of being discreet about it. Of becoming the shadow, the evil without a footprint. He crawled out and walked back to his family, leaving a mark on yet another destruction.

"Everybody! Dinner! Gabriela! Matheus! Anthony! Maria Luiza! Luiz! Come quick! It's going to get cold!" Anthony ran down, eager to see his plan in action. He sat down on the table first, securing a position as far away from his pièce de résistance as possible. He had a wide smile on his face, excited for what was about to come.

His mother innocently smiled at him as she set a steaming plate of feijoada in front of him. "My, my! I haven't ever seen you this excited to be eating feijoada!" she said.

Matheus sat on the chair right next to it. The second he rested his elbows on the table, it gave away, the leg breaking in two as the top sank to the bottom and the food began to slide off. The other legs buckled under the extra weight and creaked. Anthony's mother shrieked and tried to pick up the food as it slid down, but her attempts were in vain. Anthony's glee was written all over his face, as he stood up to admire his work. His father yelled for everyone to move away as glass plates and dishes shattered all around the remains of the table. As the rest of his family watched, horrified, Anthony's soul did a little jig.

21

Anita

She had to save Maia. She had to do it. She just couldn't seem to figure out why. *Was it because of her toys? The way she corrected me when I did or said something wrong? How she didn't care that I was filthy half the time, or that I was the maid's daughter?* But really, did it matter why? Now that she had made up her mind, was it worth spending time pondering why she wanted to save Maia? Her father had always told her that once a decision was made, there was no use revisiting the process.

She opened the file again, and looked for clues. She needed to find something, anything that she could use to trace the people who had taken her. All she had at the moment was a phone number- which was probably from a burner cell- and a name. Garcia. How much could she find out from one last name?

She opened her laptop and typed in 'Garcia' in the search bar of the browser. Within a second, several options turned up. The most famous hit was for Jerry Garcia, a guitarist from the 60s. Right underneath that, appeared the face of the man she'd met.

Aha. Anthony Garcia.

She clicked on his name, and several different links showed up at once. She clicked on the first link she found, skimmed through it. He was definitely who she was looking for.

But why the kidnap?

She went back to the main page, and clicked on News. The first hit, gave Anita her answer.

November 29

India-based CooperCoal overthrows rival Carmen Industries, replacing them to become the richest coal producing company in the world.

November 30

Carmen Industries loses multi-million dollar deal to rival Coopercoal.

She didn't bother reading the rest. She knew what she was going to find.

She opened up a new tab and looked for CooperCoal. The page opened up quickly, a host of pictures taking up most of the screen.

It was Maia's father.

She shuddered, each piece clicking together in her head, like pieces in a puzzle.

Carmen Industries was the richest coal producing company in the world.

Click

Garcia, the owner of Carmen Industries signed a multi-million-dollar contract.

Click.

Coopercoal suddenly overthrows them, becoming the richest.

Click.

Multi-million-dollar deal moves to CooperCoal, leaving Carmen Industries in the dust.

Click.

Garcia finds out and goes into a jealous rage.

Click.

He orders for something to be done- quick.

Click.

When nothing happens, he decides to go personal.

Click.

He targets CooperCoal's owner- Dev Mishra's life. His daughter is his gem, so the daughter becomes the target.

Click.

Two weeks later, Maia is gone.

Click.

Anita shut her laptop hurriedly and rubbed her face with her hands. What had she done? She put her laptop aside, and grabbed her keys from her dresser and ran out of her room.

22

Tanya

What did she see?

Tanya heard a faint knock on her door, and put her laptop aside. She flattened her dishevelled hair and smoothed out her rumpled skirt. "Come in," she called.

Shanaya poked her head in. "Hey!" she piped, opening the door wide, revealing her tall, willowy figure.

Seriously, is there anyone here who doesn't look like a model? Well there's you. A voice at the back of her head said.

Shanaya tip-toed into the room, still in her uniform. She sat down next to Tanya, smoothing the covers next to her. "How've you been holding up?" she asked gently, looking up at Tanya.

Tanya turned her eyes to the floor. How had she been holding up? Was she happy? Relieved? "I don't know," she whispered in the end, her eyes glued to the floor.

Shanaya reassuringly put her hand on Tanya's shoulder. "It'll get better you know. She'll come back," she said, her eyes reflecting the same sadness that Tanya had in hers. "You know what makes me feel better whenever I'm sad?" Shanaya said, cheery again. "A nice, long walk. Wanna come with?" She walked towards the door.

Tanya rolled her eyes and smiled. She stood up and followed Shanaya, locking the door behind her.

✳✳✳

The leaves rustled in the wind, and Tanya pulled her jacket closer, enjoying the comfortable silence that Shanaya and she had been sharing.

"It's getting colder eh?" Shanaya said.

"Yeah. It's a cold winter this time," Tanya replied. *Are you sure it's not your heart that's cold?*

"It's really great to see you back at school by the way. The pressure is a great way to get your mind off of things."

"Yeah, I guess," Tanya said off-handedly. She wanted to go back to her room. She could hear her laptop pining for her. "You know what? I think I'll go back now. Thanks for letting me come with you," Tanya said hurriedly and spun around.

Shanaya caught her elbow, laughing. "Oh not so fast sister. You're coming to dinner," Shanaya said.

Tanya inwardly groaned. Since she'd restarted school, she had been avoiding the cafeteria. She'd been living off of biscuit packets and ready-to-eat noodles. She could avoid people in class, that was no problem- but the cafeteria, which was the school hangout area- was danger zone. "Uhh, I don't think so," Tanya said with uncertainty, trying to break free from Shanaya's tight grasp.

"If you're worried about people treating you weirdly, I'll take care of it. Just stick by my side, and you'll be absolutely question free!" she said, satisfactorily clapping her hands together.

"No."

"Yes."

"No."

"Yes."

Tanya huffed in defeat. "Fine," she muttered, and began to trudge along.

Shanaya strolled along in front of her, waving to people on the way.

Tanya kept her shoulders hunched, letting her hair fall loose over her face.

She smelt the cafeteria before she saw it. The smell of fresh paneer butter masala wafted through the large glass doors. Tanya lifted her nose appreciatively, sniffing the air. *Food. Real food.* Her stomach growled in anticipation.

Shanaya laughed and opened the doors to the cafeteria. She sashayed inside, leaving Tanya in her wake.

As soon as she took a single step, it was as if though her one step had been amplified 200 times around the room. Everyone stopped what they were doing and looked up at her. Mustering up all the courage she had left in her body, she said, "Take a picture, it'll last longer."

Everyone looked at their plates, although someone at the far end actually did take a picture. They went back to their usual chatter, forgetting all about her.

Shanaya walked back to Tanya and linked their arms together. "Look, I told you everything would be okay! Come on, let's get some real food in you." Shanaya said, as she guided Tanya through the tables, towards the cafeteria line.

They headed over to a large table off to the side of the cafeteria with their food trays. As she sat down, Tanya looked longingly over at the largest table in the centre, where she used to usually sit with Maia. The table she now sat at consisted of people that she could only describe as artsy. The girl opposite to her had wild hair, the ends of it looking like it had been flung through a rainbow. Another boy seemed to be air,

Is he playing the saxophone? God, I need to get out of here.

"Everyone, this is Tanya! She's sitting with us today!" Shanaya said, waving her hands in the air so as to catch everyone's attention.

No one even batted an eyelash.

Shanaya shrugged.

"What can I say? They're not really used to newcomers."

"Oh, that's no problem." Tanya replied. She shovelled food into her mouth as fast as she could, barely tasting what she was eating. With the last mouthful, Tanya swung her legs over the bench and picked up her tray. "I should get going now. Thanks. For everything," she said and walked away before Shanaya could protest. Disposing her tray, Tanya weaved her way through the crowd once again, and swung open the door.

She stepped into the chilly wind and made her way to the dorms. It was a long walk. She jumped over a few bushes skillfully to get to her room faster, and finally saw the square building in front of her. It was completely dark and silent, not a whisper or giggle heard. Everyone was at dinner. Tanya smiled, and climbed up to her room.

As soon as she locked her door behind her, she jumped onto her bed and opened her laptop. The footage started. She fast forwarded a little until Anita walked back into the room. She seemed to be looking for something, and a few seconds later walked straight towards where the camera was positioned. Tanya heart began to race, her eyes widening with every step.

Anita picked up the camera, her face taking up the whole screen. "Meet me day after tomorrow at five at the park near your school. For your own good - and hers."

∗

Anita

Growing up amongst hundreds of other people just like her, in shacks made of asbestos held strong by gossip, if there was one feeling Anita was used to, it was the feeling of being watched. She had grown up with eyes all around her, tracking her every move, from old to young. Later when she moved into a big house, she felt a stark absence of that feeling. The loneliness nagged at her, so she irrationally had large windows built, as if to compensate for the lack of people around her.

But now, Anita suddenly felt that welcoming feeling again. She woke up at night, with the feeling that she was being watched. Although the curtains were drawn, she couldn't shake the feeling off. She lifted her head up and scanned the room. She quietly slipped her hand to her dresser, where she kept her gun. She was always extra cautious the days before and after a case. She scanned the room again, and a small red light caught her eye. A camera. Anita's heart started beating fast, as she sat up rubbing her eyes, pretending as though nothing were wrong. There had to be a way to find out who the camera belonged to without jeopardizing her safety. She walked towards the window and sat down at the windowsill right next to where the camera was. She opened the curtains to let the moonlight in, and made sure that her face was out of the camera's range. She took her phone out of her pyjama pocket and opened the camera. There was a tiny piece of masking tape on top of the camera. Anita zoomed in on her phone to see what it said.

Tan-tan

Anger bubbled up inside Anita. Who did that little good-for-nothing think she was? How dare she? Anita had to make her pay. She drew the curtains closed and went back to bed. She had the perfect plan.

23

Maia

It had been at least a week. At least that's what she thought. And still, no one came to her rescue. She didn't like thinking this way- thinking that she needed to be saved, that she was a damsel in distress. But still, why hadn't anyone found her yet? And why exactly was she here?

Flicking away a fly that sat on her arm, she stared at the plate of food in front of her. It was *sambar* rice today. Maia's upper lip curled in distaste as she noted its revolting yellow colour. *I need to get out of here. Quick.* It had been three days since the second man came to talk to her. Since then, she'd had no human contact.

Rays of light shone through the windows, dust particles clearly visible. She stood up, wincing as pain shot up her leg and walked towards one of the windows. She peeped through the biggest hole she could find, straining her eyes to recognise her surroundings. She saw green and brown, and could hear the faint rustling of leaves.

Forest. I'm in a forest.

She hobbled to the door, and tried it, with no luck. It was bolted from the outside. Sighing, she made her way back to the makeshift bed and sat down, racking her brains for an escape. She couldn't pull off anything that required jumping, her leg wouldn't be able to take it. So, an escape through the windows was out. That left the doors. She had to figure out a way to get them open.

Her eyes scanned the shed once again, falling on the plate of food. An idea went off in her head like a light bulb. If there was food getting in, it had to be getting out. And since the plates from yesterday weren't in the shed, someone had to be coming in and taking it. The food was always there when she woke up every morning, so it had to be coming during the night. Which meant that sometime in the night, the door opened. If she stayed up long enough, she could be awake at the time the person came in, and could possibly make her escape.

✳✳✳

. The day moved slowly, as days tend to when one has nothing to do. She spent much of her time gazing at the ceiling, hoping to conserve as much energy as possible without falling asleep. As the sun started to set, her heart started beating faster. When and if she could escape, what would she do after? If she was in a forest, how far would she have to run before she found signs of habitation? There was no forest close to anywhere she knew. How far would she be able to run, with a busted leg? She shook her head, focusing on getting back home, where she belonged.

But is that where you really belong? Is home where you belong when the people you share the home with are most probably why you're here?

The voice at the back of her head added to Maia's discomfort.

You don't know that; you don't know that they're the reason I'm here.

She fought back.

Oh, so you suppose you're here for you? It became pretty obvious it was about them when the two men came in.

Maia kept quiet, having no answer to her own inner demons. She fiddled with her bracelet, the shiny diamonds catching what little light there was in the room, coming from the sole broken light bulb above her, and one in the far end of the shed. It had been a gift from her parents on her 12th birthday. Or it might have been a 'we're sorry we missed another important event' bracelet. She couldn't remember anymore. She had been so worried about the things she could hold that she had forgotten what it was like to feel.

Her eyelids drooped, but she fought to keep them open. Her stomach rumbled in protest, as she wearily eyed the abandoned sambar rice at the foot of her bed.

Can't be too long now, she thought, nervously twiddling her thumbs together.

Maia's eyes were starting to burn, when she heard a low, creaking sound, and saw the gate open a fraction of an inch. All her sleep gone, she hastily got up and tiptoed her way to the corner of the large door, clenching her hands into fists. A large metal tray entered first, and Maia slowly moved forward. As soon as she saw the tiniest strip of skin, she pounced on the person, colliding with a warm and large body as both of them fell to the floor with a soft thud. Without wasting any time, she hastily stood up and tried to make a run for it. She felt a warm hand wrap around her wrist and pull her back to the floor.

Maia cried out in pain as her body came into contact with the hard ground. She backed away from the person, her eyes wide with fear. She stood up unsteadily, and the person stood up as well, brushing the invisible dirt off her black pants. The person was a short and stocky woman in her late thirties.

"Look, I have to get out. Please let me go, please," Maia pleaded, clasping her hands in front of her. "Please, Marie," she said, reading the nametag.

The woman ignored her, and placed the plate of food on the floor. She turned around without a word, and began to walk out.

Maia felt a flurry of panic rise in her chest. She limped forward and grabbed the woman's hand. "Please." The desperation was evident in her eyes.

The woman sighed and turned around, shutting the gate behind her. She twisted her hand free of Maia's iron grip and folded her arms. "What do you want? I can't help you get out," she said.

"Then just tell me why I'm here," she said.

The woman eyed Maia's wrist. "I'm not doing it for free," she said in a straight voice.

After a second, Maia realised what she was talking about. She unclipped her bracelet and held it out. "Here, have it, please. Just tell me what I need to know."

The woman took her bracelet with a smile.

24

Vineeta

"Mummy! Mama! Where are you? I can't find you!" A 4-year-old Maia giggled, as she scampered around the large living room. She stopped and tapped her chin. Her face was scrunched up in thought, and Vineeta covered her mouth to stop the laughter. Suddenly, Maia's whole face smoothed out, and she broke into a bright smile. She ran to where Vineeta hid, and poked her back. "Caught you!" she giggled.

Vineeta laughed along, pulling her close.

"I love you Mummy." Maia said, as she wrung her small arms around her mother's neck.

Vineeta sighed. "Oh, I love you too, honey."

✳✳✳

"Dev! Dev! You forgot the purple balloons! She has to have purple balloons at her birthday party!" Vineeta cried as she bustled around the room.

"I got pink instead! Same thing! How does it matter?" Dev shrugged, as he put up streamers on the other side of the room.

Vineeta spun around. "Dev, her dress is purple! Everything in this room is purple! How can her balloons be pink?!" she exclaimed. "She's turning six, and it's her last birthday party in London! Everything has to be perfect!"

Dev laughed. "Okay, okay, I'll go get the balloons."

Two hours later, Maia ran into the room, her friends behind her. She was wearing a long purple gown, paired with a purple tiara, and purple shoes that had taken Vineeta and Dev days to find. Maia's face glowed, as she clasped her hands together. Catching sight of her parents, she ran to them and hugged them. "Thank you thank you thank you! It's perfect!" she squealed.

✳✳✳

"You're missing my recital. That's why you bothered to call. I've been practicing all year, and you're missing it," Maia said quietly.

Vineeta pushed the phone closer to her ear, struggling to hear her daughter. "Sorry dear. We tried our best, but we just couldn't find any flights and-"

"You have your own plane!" Maia yelled.

"Maia, you need to be rational here. We can't just get the plane out on such short notice-" Vineeta began.

"Short notice?! I told you four months ago, Mum! Was that short notice for you? Should I book an appointment next time?" Maia cried, her sobs audible three continents away.

"We're on important business here, and anyways, at least Pratiksha will be there right?" Vineeta said lightly.

"Pratiksha isn't enough! She works for us! You're my parents, I'm not an adult yet! I'm only fourteen; I can't live without my parents!" Maia screeched.

A man stuck his head out from inside the meeting room.

"Mrs. Mishra, you're needed inside," he said and disappeared.

Vineeta sighed. "Maia, I have to go. I'm sorry. Dad and I will make it up to you. I promise," she said.

"Don't make promises you can't keep," Maia hissed, as she cut the line.

***

"Maia? We're home!" Dev shouted, as the driver pulled in the last suitcase. They heard an audible gasp from upstairs, and a figure came flying down the stairs and crashed into them.

"You're home, you're home, you're home, you're really home!" Maia exclaimed as she let her parents free from her grip.

Dev's phone buzzed in his pocket. "I have to take this," he muttered, and walked into the dining room.

"Oh Mum, I have soo much to show you and Dad! I re-decorated my room, I got a few more medals, I took some really cool pictures..." Maia gushed.

Vineeta smiled. "Oh honey, that's great!"

Dev walked back into the room, putting his phone back in his pocket. "Vineeta, we have to go," he said, looking cautiously at Maia.

Maia's face fell. "So soon?" she asked. "But you just got here!"

"I know, but we really have to go. Sorry. We'll see you at dinner," Dev said, as Vineeta threw Maia an equally sad smile, and left the house behind her husband, leaving a distraught daughter in their wake.

✳✳✳

Vineeta jerked awake, the covers wrapped tight around her body.

Maia.

She shut her eyes tightly, and watched the phosphenes dance in front of her eyes, and disappear one by one. Her husband was on the seat next to hers- sound asleep unaware of any disturbances. "Dev," she whispered, shaking his arm. "Dev, wake up," she whispered again, shaking him harder.

He groaned, turning over. Seeing the look on Vineeta's face, he immediately shot up, facing her. "What happened?" he asked, concern flashing across his face.

"We need to see Tanya. She'll know something," Vineeta said frantically. She began to pull the covers out from under her, but Dev gently pushed her back onto the bed.

"You said you already spoke to her?" Dev asked.

"I did. But I have this strange feeling. I'm so scared it's happening. What are we going to do? We need to go see her."

"I think it might be happening too," Dev rubbed his face with his hands. "This is completely uncharacteristic. But we're on a plane Vinny. We'll go the second we land." Dev said lightly. He bent over and kissed her forehead.

Vineeta's eyelids fluttered. "Okay," Vineeta breathed, and let sleep hold her in its tight grasp.

✳✳✳

Dev and Vineeta were out as soon as the plane doors opened.

"Dev! Dev, let's go! They don't have school today and I want to get there in case Tanya decides to go out anywhere," Vineeta whispered, as they rushed through immigration.

"Ramesh should be waiting with the car," Dev said. "We'll have the bags sent over to the house later."

They left the airport and were welcomed by their driver Ramesh.

"Go to the school. As fast as you can," Dev said. Dev looked at Vineeta. "What do you think we're going to find?" he asked her softly.

"Something. Anything. She has to know something. She was in school for heaven's sake. What kind of safety does a school have if they can lose a student on campus?" Vineeta replied, even softer, staring at the floor.

Dev looked away, out of the window. "Tell me Ramesh, when you took her to school that morning, did she seem different?" Dev asked the driver.

Ramesh looked at the two through the rear-view mirror. "No ma'am, sir. She seemed perfectly normal, a little excited rather. She kept typing on her phone, in between her naps but I suppose that's normal enough for her," he said, his eyes returning to the road, as he drove down the narrowing roads that opened up to the large school gates.

At the sight of the school sticker on the windshield, the gates opened, and the car glided through, into the large school premises. The car came to a halt in front of the Administrative Department.

"Good luck sir and ma'am." Ramesh said, his voices tinged with sadness. Dev vaguely nodded, his eyes focused on the large building in front of them. Vineeta stepped out as well, patting down her hair. Both of them glanced at each other as the car rolled away, and moved towards the entrance. The doors automatically slid open, revealing a colourful yet professional-looking room.

There were several multi-coloured sofas and armchairs, with numerous paintings dotting the walls. At one end, taking up one whole wall was the large reception. Vineeta and Dev walked across the carpeted floor, straight to the desk.

"Hi, my name is Dev Mishra. I'm Maia Mishra's father. Is there any way we can meet Tanya Sharma?"

"I'm sorry sir, we cannot allow outsiders apart from family to meet students right now. We've tightened security."

Too little too late.

"I understand that, but can you please try? It's really important. She may have important clues as to where our daughter is."

The receptionist looked down for a second. "Let me see what I can do," she said, picking up her phone.

Dev and Vineeta nodded in gratitude.

The receptionist hung up and looked at them. "The Principal is not on campus currently, but I have permission to allow Tanya to come here to speak to you. You can take one of the sofas here. She will probably take a few minutes to come here."

"Thank you very much." Both of them moved towards the sofas.

Ten minutes later, the wide reception doors opened and Tanya walked in. Vineeta felt something in the pit of her stomach as Tanya gave them a wry smile and sat across from them.

"Hello Auntie, Uncle."

"Hi Tanya, how are you doing?" Dev said, giving Vineeta a warning look.

Tanya shrugged. "I've been better."

Vineeta leaned forward. "I feel like we didn't get to speak properly over the phone. Is there anything you aren't telling us Tanya? Please, please think about it. Did you really tell us everything?"

Tanya bit her lip and didn't meet their eyes. "Well, not exactly."

Vineeta's knuckles turned white against the armrest of the sofa. She tried to keep her voice from rising. "What did you leave out?"

"A few weeks ago, she met this guy on Twitter-"

"A guy?" Dev repeated.

"Yes. A guy. They started talking and they really seemed to hit it off. She would be talking to him like all the time. He's our age, and goes to school somewhere here in the city. She was going on a date that night. That's why she stayed over, because it would be easier to leave-"

"You *helped* her?" Vineeta asked incredulously.

The receptionist looked up at them.

"He DM'd saying that they were going to meet at a restaurant somewhere close by and I was supposed to wait around there so that we could go back together," Tanya continued, appearing to have not heard Vineeta. "But when we got there, he had arranged for a picnic instead. So they went to a field nearby and I was waiting at the side the entire time."

"And then?" Dev asked, his hand trembling.

"It was getting really late, so I texted Maia and said she should wrap up, but then she came over to me, and she had like this wild look in her eyes. I had never seen it before. She said she wanted to run away. Just leave. I tried to convince her otherwise, but she was adamant. I told her I was going to call you guys but she did the weirdest thing. She took her phone, took out her sim card and just broke it in half. She said she needed to do this, and that maybe one day she'd come back, but that I needn't wait. And that was it."

"Why didn't you try harder to stop her? You're her best friend."

"I-I don't know."

Vineeta huffed in frustration. "You said they used to speak on Twitter?"

"Y-yes. At least that's what she told me."

"And do you know anything else about this boy? What's his name?"

"Um, Ayaan, I think." Tanya had begun to fidget nervously, and would not meet their eyes.

"Last name?"

"No clue."

"Did she tell you anything else before she went? Where she was going? When she would be back?" Dev asked, a tone of urgency in his voice.

"No."

"And you're sure she ran away with him? This Ayaan boy?"

"I-Maybe. I don't know. I don't think she would've. He probably just planted the idea in her head."

"Can you tell us the name of the restaurant they went to?"

Tanya's eyes widened. "Um, I don't remember right now. I'll text it to you one second." She went on her phone and typed furiously for a few seconds, until Vineeta's phone buzzed. "There. I sent it."

Dev put his head in his hands. He gave Vineeta a resigned look. "Let's go Vinny. We need to find a way to read these chats. Maybe we can find out more about this boy then. Thanks Tanya. We'll see you later."

Vineeta slumped back in her chair, all life draining out of her. She kept repeating the same words over and over- *run away, run away, she wanted to run away* - like a chant, as if that would somehow make Maia magically reappear. Vineeta knew, that as soon as she looked into her husband's eyes, the tears would fall out again, and this time, she would not be able to control herself. "How did this happen?" Vineeta asked, her voice soft.

"No Vinny. Something's wrong here. Maia would never make rash decisions like this. Especially not ones that could jeopardise her life and future."

Vineeta looked at Dev. "What if she's following in our footsteps? If I recall correctly you made a similar kind of rash decision when you were just a little older."

Dev gave her a sharp look. "That was different Vineeta. You know it was. I don't like to talk about it." He stood up and motioned for her to stand.

"Where are we going?" she muttered.

"Tech department." Dev replied. "I want to read these chats. There's no way Maia would hide anything from us. She's told us about every boy she has ever liked before. I don't see how this is different."

"Maybe she's growing up. Maybe she's not as comfortable anymore."

"Still, I need to see. We can try to retrace her steps."

Vineeta nodded, as they exited the building and made their way towards the main cluster of buildings.

"Administration, Faculty, Humanities, World Language, Science, there it is, Tech! That's where we need to go." Dev said, as he pulled Vineeta towards the entrance.

They walked into the building and down the long corridor before stopping in front of a door. *Avneet Krishnan: Head of Technology.*   Vineeta knocked on the door twice, sharing a concerned look with her husband.

"Come in." A voice rang from inside, as Vineeta wrapped her hand against the warm doorknob, and twisted it.

The first thing that Vineeta saw- smelt rather- was the incense. There were sticks everywhere, the wisps of smoke merging together to create an odd fragrance that spread around the room. A man sat on a large table directly in front of them, typing away on a laptop. He was in his late-forties, but wisps of grey coloured his otherwise dark hair, making him seem much older. He was well-dressed, in an expensive navy blue suit and an Omega watch gleaming on his wrist. A look of surprise flashed across his face for a second when he glanced up at his visitors. "Can I help you?" he asked, standing up.

"I hope so, Sir. My name is Dev Mishra. This is my wife Vineeta. We are Maia Mishra's parents. We need a little technical support. We would go to other people, but it's urgent."

"No problem, Sir. We are all deeply affected by Maia's disappearance and we only hope she comes back to us as soon as possible," Mr. Krishnan said, shaking their hands, sounding well-rehearsed. He gestured for them to take a seat. "How can I help you?"

"It has come to our knowledge that Maia was speaking to someone on Twitter for a few weeks. We want to go through those and see if it can provide us with any clues as to who he is or where we can find him."

"That will not be a problem at all. Unfortunately, we cannot track any IP addresses, but we'll help you to the best of our capabilities. Please follow me."

"Thank you," Vineeta said as they made their way out of the office and into a large computer lab in the adjacent room.

"Please have a seat. Do you know Maia's Twitter password?"

Vineeta and Dev looked at each other helplessly. "I think I know," Vineeta said.

Mr. Krishnan nodded and turned the computer screen towards Vineeta. "Please go ahead."

Vineeta uncertainly began to type. Within a second, the account was verified. She let go of a breath she didn't remember holding, as a small smile played on Dev's lips.

"She still uses the same password, doesn't she?" he said.

"Always londontown45. Ever since I can remember. I keep telling her she'll have to stop depending on that one password as she grows up," Vineeta replied, with tears in her eyes.

They went to Maia's DMs and found the chat with Ayaan. Vineeta felt strange reading through them, it felt like a gross invasion of privacy, even though it was her own daughter.

"Wait a minute. Vinny, stop, go up," Dev said, leaning forward.

"What is it?" Vineeta asked scrolling up.

"Look. This doesn't match what Tanya said. She said they were going to a restaurant. This says they met on an airstrip. Why did she lie?"

"That doesn't make any sense. Maybe their plans changed later? Let's see," Vineeta said scrolling down.

As they reached the end, a chill ran down Vineeta's spine at the last message.

@ayaan_gupta: Sorry I couldn't make it today darling. I have a proper reason though, don't worry about that. You see, the thing is, I don't exist.

Surprise! You didn't see that one coming, did you? I have to admit, it was hilarious watching you fall for someone who isn't even real. Sorry, but not really.

~T

"That's why she lied," Vineeta said in a low voice.

"What does that mean then? Is it what we think it is?" Dev asked, his voice trembling.

25

Maia

"Wake up. Wake up." A voice repeated, shaking her stiff shoulders, and ridding her of her blanket.

Maia jolted up, alert. For a moment she thought she was back home, and her maid was shaking her awake. But her room was never so dimly lit, she had never been awoken in the middle of the night, and her maid's hands had never been so rough. She rubbed her eyes. She was still in the shed, and it was Marie who was shaking her awake. "What?" Maia asked, her voice on the edge of whiny.

Marie pushed a few strands of hair off her face, Maia's diamond bracelet glinting. "Food." Marie pushed a plate of food towards her.

"Did you find out anything?"

"This is kidnap."

"I'm well aware."

"By a big white man. He doesn't come to Bangalore often. But when he does, Dube Sir stops being nice to us housekeeping staff. Too stressful, I think."

Dube. The first man. "Do you know his first name?" Maia asked, racking her brain. That last name sounded really familiar.

"No."

Maia sighed. "Well do you know anything else?

"I hear something about police. I was passing by and the white man said, 'they will know not to call the police'."

"What does that mean?"

"I don't know. That's all I know." With that, Marie got up to leave.

Suddenly Maia grabbed her hand. "Oh, not so fast. You're taking me with you." Maia suddenly felt a sharp pain on her left side, and saw everything go black.

26

Tanya

Tanya jolted awake, her sheets twisted around her, beads of sweat rolling down her face. She had fallen asleep in her day clothes, and the belt hoops of her jeans were digging into her skin. Her alarm clock beeped 2:18 a.m. She'd been asleep for only 2 hours. She couldn't get Maia's parents' faces out of her head. They looked so small, so miserable. In her mind, successful people had always been happy. At least, that's what she was banking on. As her mind ran through the conversation with Maia's parents, she mentally kicked herself. Why did she tell them about the Twitter thing? They would surely find out she was lying. The entire restaurant thing was a lie. They would obviously find a way to read through the chats and be back in no time. She picked up her phone and opened the fake account to see how incriminating the evidence was. Her heart stopped as she read the last message. She might as well have put a picture of herself.

How could you have been so stupid? You could have said anything else- come up with anything else. The voice at the back of her screamed, deafening her. She was done for. Tanya covered her ears with her hands, trying to block it out. She rubbed her eyes, swinging her legs out of bed. She stood up, unsteady on her feet, and moved towards the bathroom. Her phone glowed in the darkness and beeped four times, indicating that Tanya had received a new message. She went over to it, crouching down to where it lay on the floor, charging.

Unknown Number

I hope you haven't forgotten about our little rendezvous today. Don't be late.

A chill ran down Tanya's spine. How had Anita found her number? She shut her phone off and threw it towards her bed. Her eyes burned and the whole world blurred. "What have I done? What have I done?" she whispered to herself. She pressed the sides of her head with her hands, trying to push the weight of guilt off her head. Pain shot through her head, blocking her thought process.

She stood up and moved towards her dresser in a daze. She fiddled with the handles, and pulled the topmost one open roughly. She sifted through the clutter of objects stuffed inside, until her hands found the wadded-up notes stuffed in the corner. She took them out, counting them with her fingers. 2, 4, 6, 8. Perfect. She picked out two of the four crinkled 2000- rupee notes and stuffed them in the back pocket of her jeans. She quietly unlocked her door, and crept out soundlessly.

As soon as she left her building, she broke into a run, swiftly darting down the dark pathways of the school grounds. She could move through this place with her eyes closed. She reached the hole, carefully picking it apart and slipping out. She broke into a run again, looking around, to see if anyone was following her.

Fifteen minutes later, she put her hands on her knees panting. She stood in front of the only lit store on the street. Everyday Liquors. She pushed her way to the counter, through a throng of people, and shouted to the store owner in Hindi, "One bottle of beer."

"Branded or local?" he yelled back.

"Doesn't matter. Actually branded," she said again, rubbing her eyes. Someone patted her on the back. She turned around, and saw the face of a drunk man dangerously close to hers. She recoiled in disgust, and slapped him on the cheek. With a hand on his cheek, he moved backwards, a look of betrayal on his face. Tanya rolled her eyes and turned back, to see a large beer bottle in front of her. She slapped a note on the counter.

Tucking the bottle under her arm, she stepped out of the store. She walked slowly, letting the wind catch her hair in little tufts. She walked up the hill, where the school fence was, and sat in front of it. She lifted the bottle to her mouth, and began to chug it down. She stopped to take a breath, the bitter liquid burning her throat. She put the bottle next to her, and rolled it, so that it tumbled down, and crashed on the concrete pavement. She giggled, feeling lightheaded. She stood up, nearly tripping over her own feet. "Oo, careful Tan-Tan. We don't want to fall do we? Noo, that would be a disaster. After all, you have a very important meeting today remember?" Giggling, she hobbled away towards her dorm room.

The cool wind didn't help her at all, but only muddled her up further. She touched every lamp on the way, giggling as she named them. She finally reached her building, squinting from the bright light, before staggering up the stairs. She had left her door unlocked when she had left. She pushed it open with her foot, and stepped inside. "Man, the floor looks real good," she mumbled, shutting the door with her foot, and tumbling to the floor.

"Night night."

27

Anita

"Ma'am, is this for a specific occasion?" the saleswoman asked, fingering her ID card.

Anita tapped her finger on her chin thoughtfully, eyeing the array of lipsticks set out in front of her. "What colour do you suggest for a super-secret meeting to discuss a high-profile kidnapping?" she said. Seeing the look on the sales woman's face, Anita laughed. "I'm just joking. Calm down," she said with a smile.

The saleswoman smiled. "I suggest our newest colour. It's a dark red, and it will go very well with your skin tone. Would you like to test a sample?" the woman asked, reaching out to pick up a dark red coloured tube. She handed Anita the tube, uncapping it for her.

Anita drew a smear across her hand, and examined it carefully. "Yup okay. That's perfect. I'll take it," she said, rubbing the smear off with a tissue. She glanced at her watch as she paid for the lipstick.

3:45

Perfect

***

Anita made her way to a small clearing in the midst of trees, pushing her hair back.

Tanya had arrived before her, and had her head in her hands.

Anita made her way to the bench and seated herself.

Tanya continued to massage her temple, unaware of Anita's presence.

Anita cleared her throat.

Tanya jumped. "Oh. You're here," she said.

Anita raised her eyebrows.

Suddenly, Tanya leaned towards her, and whispered, "Maia's parents came to visit me yesterday. They seemed unsuspecting at the beginning, but now I think they're onto me. I was such an idiot I told them about the Twitter thing. I seriously think they know I did something. Oh god, how could I have been so stupid? And-" Her voice lowered further, "I think I'm being followed. Since this morning, I feel like someone's been watching me. And don't tell me I'm being paranoid. I know someone is. I don't think I should stay here much longer. I have to go." Tanya stood up, but Anita grasped her hand tightly.

"*Sit,*" she whispered menacingly, and Tanya obliged, her eyes darting from side to side. "You don't even know why I called you here. See, the thing is, I changed my mind."

"I don't believe you." Tanya said.

"Don't look at me like it's not possible. I...I found out about some things. And, I've changed my mind."

Tanya brought her disbelieving gaze back to Anita.

"Well, you could think that way, because that would certainly explain why I want to get her out."

Tanya leaned forward slowly. "What do you mean? You know where she is?"

"You don't need to know any details right now" Anita said

Tanya huffed in frustration, and Anita noticed her leg jumping up and down nervously.

Anita began to rethink her decision. Did she really need Tanya? Couldn't she do this by herself? No, a voice at the back of her head told her, *you need her. If it comes to that, you don't want to go down alone, do you?* "Do you want in or not? Can you imagine the glory, when we find her? Your name, splashed across the papers, news channels, everywhere you could imagine? Isn't that what you always wanted? Acceptance? For everyone to look at you, like you've done everything just right?"

Tanya looked down, biting her lip. "Fine. I'll do it," she said, her voice wavering.

Satisfied with herself, Anita stood up. "Good. You'll hear from me, very, very soon." She picked up her bag, and began to walk away.

Click.

Anita froze. She looked back at Tanya, her eyes wide.

Someone had taken a picture of their little rendezvous.

*

Tanya

No. No, please, this can't be happening.

28

Vineeta

Vineeta was sitting on an armchair, her eyes fixated on a spot on the wall.

"Madam?" A voice came from behind her, making her jump.

She stood up, and straightened her skirt. "Yes Ramesh? Did you find anything?" she enquired, as her husband walked in.

"Find what?" he asked.

Vineeta's heart lurched with sudden fear.

"Um... Dev! No-nothing, I was just - it's nothing," she stammered, trying to usher Dev out.

"No, wait-wait, Ramesh what's going on? Vinny, stop," Dev said, prying Vineeta's hands off his shoulders.

Ramesh stood uncomfortably, fingering the camera in his hands.

Leaving Vineeta behind, Dev walked up to Ramesh, and held his hand out for the camera. "What did she tell you to do?" he asked.

Ramesh shifted his weight from one foot to another, as Vineeta gave him a pleading look. "Um...Sir, actually-" he began.

"Just get to the point," Dev cut in.

"Well, Madam asked me to-"

Vineeta sighed. "Stop, Ramesh. Dev, I told him to follow Tanya. It's partly her fault Maia's gone. She can't be trusted. I need to know what she knows."

Dev massaged his temples. "Ramesh, what did you find?" he asked.

Both Vineeta and Dev moved towards Ramesh, who took the camera from Dev and turned it on. "Yesterday, she was meeting with someone in a park by their school. I got there just in time. The park is huge, I lost her for a second and then I couldn't find her again. By the time I got there, the other woman was just about to leave, and I got this picture right before the other woman walked away. In fact, one of the pictures I got, she's looking in the direction of the camera." He stopped at a picture that showed the back of a bench. Tanya was seated on it, her face tilted in the direction of the other person, and she had a faraway look in her eyes. The other woman's head was turned directly towards the camera.

Dev looked at Vineeta. "Do you think this had something to do with the account?" he asked softly, his eyes fixed on the picture.

"It has to be. But who is she? Do you think she's the one behind all of this?" Vineeta said. She turned to Ramesh. "Thank you,Ramesh, you may leave. And remember to drop off those papers I'd given you earlier at the office."

Ramesh nodded and walked out, as Vineeta sank back into the chair, her hands over her eyes. "Despicable isn't it? Even when our daughter lies God knows where, we have to continue working. She could be starving, for all we know, and still. Still, we are managing a blasted company. We couldn't even protect our own daughter. How are we supposed to protect a global company?" she spat bitterly. What kind of mother had she become?

At first, running away seemed bad enough, but now that they knew about the fake account, Dev and Vineeta were at a dead end. If Ayaan never existed, then that meant that Maia didn't run away with him. But then where had she gone? And now, who was this other woman? What did she have to do with Tanya?

"I need to get out of this house. I'm going for a drive," Vineeta said, standing up.

Dev walked out of the room, muttering to himself.

She walked out of the family room, and climbed the stairs. The wall next to her was adorned with family photos, all of them organised chronologically. Vineeta touched the left end of each photo, a habit from the past. She changed hurriedly and grabbed her keys. She drove away from her house and onto the main road in shiny black Jaguar, gliding past all the other cars, and gaping people.

Is that the woman who is in the newspaper? The one who owns the company?

She imagined some of them saying.

Look at her car! She must be made of money. The others would say.

She had learned to ignore all of these people, especially the press. The best advice she'd ever been given was to ignore the press.

Vineeta looked around her. She seemed to have arrived in a more crowded part of the city. There was a large market around her, and people bustled around, too much in a hurry to notice Vineeta. She drove through the milling streets aimlessly, swerving through vendors. All of a sudden, a woman appeared in front of her. The woman tried to move backwards and out of the way. At the same time, Vineeta swerved, nearly hitting a lamp post. The woman tripped and fell on the road in a cloud of dust with a muffled scream. Vineeta gasped and stopped her car, rushing out of it. The woman was clutching her leg in pain.

"Oh my God. I am so sorry. We need to get you to a hospital!" she said to the woman in Kannada and helped her up.

The woman hobbled along, one arm around Vineeta's shoulders. "Madam, it's okay. I'm fine," the woman replied, wincing.

Vineeta shook her head, and helped the woman into the backseat of the car, with no thoughts to the leather seats. A crowd of people had gathered around the car. Vineeta shooed them away with a wave of her hand. She drove towards the nearest hospital she knew, taking it easy over the rough road and potholes.

She looked at the woman in the backseat through the rear-view mirror. Something about her struck Vineeta as oddly familiar, but she couldn't place a finger on it. She combed through the memories in her head, trying to figure out how she knew the woman. But it was impossible. In her line, she met hundreds of new people every day and it was impossible to keep track of them. "Do I know you?" she asked in Kannada.

The other woman chuckled, catching her breath when her laugh hurt her sides. "You don't recognise me, do you?" she asked. When Vineeta shook her head, she said, "Chetana, madam. I used to clean you house almost ten years ago."

Vineeta gasped in remembrance. "Chetana! You look so different now!"

Ten years ago, Chetana had been scrawny and malnutritioned. The Chetana in her back seat had gained several pounds, and had a healthy glow to her face. She wore an expensive sari, in contrast to the drab and cheap ones she wore earlier.

"Yes, I have changed quite a bit. Thanks to my daughter," she replied, massaging the sides of her leg.

"Is your leg getting worse?" Vineeta asked, concerned. When Chetana shook her head, she continued, "Speaking of your daughter, how is she? She would be about what, 25, 26 now?"

"Anita's very well. She brings in a lot of money, which is very helpful."

Vineeta nodded approvingly. "What does she do?"

Chetana frowned. "Actually Madam, I'm not too sure. She doesn't speak of it much, and never replies to my questions if I ask her anything about it."

Vineeta drove the car to the Emergency Room entrance and called for paramedics to take Chetana in. Chetana protested, saying that the bleeding had stopped and she was fine now, but Vineeta wouldn't hear her. After Chetana was put in a wheelchair, Vineeta parked the car and rushed inside. Vineeta's nose protested against the smell of hospital. She moved to Chetana's bed, where her wound was being treated.

Chetana smiled at her gratefully, then took something out of the waistband of her sari. "Madam, can you call my daughter? I simply don't understand how to use these new phones." Vineeta chuckled and took her phone and unlocked it.

"You need to password-protect this Chetana! Times aren't good anymore!' Vineeta said as she searched through the name list for Anita's contact. She pressed call, and handed the phone to Chetana.

"Arre, Madam you should talk to her, she will like it. She was asking about you the other day."

Vineeta smiled. "While I'm sure that would be lovely, this is not the time for reunions."

Chetana spoke to Anita in a hushed voice as Vineeta looked at the time. It was getting late. "Madam, she will be here soon. You need not stay," Chetana said, hanging up.

"You're sure you'll be fine?" Chetana nodded, and Vineeta wished her a speedy recovery.

***

That Night

Vineeta's phone glowed and rang. "Hello?"

"If you're smart enough, you know who I am," a voice said menacingly through the speaker.

Vineeta's blood ran cold. She'd heard that voice in countless interviews. Anthony Garcia. "Also, if you're smart enough, you should have figured out by now that I have your daughter. If you want her back, you need to do one simple thing. Sell the company. To us, and I give you your daughter. As simple as that. Contact the police, and the next place you'll be going to is a graveyard to bid your little girl goodbye. You have three days." The line cut.

Vineeta's heart began to race. They looked at each other, eyes wide open in shock.

"Do you know what this means?" he said. "She didn't just leave. She was kidnapped. Our worst fears have come true."

29

Anita

"I don't get it! I asked you to do one thing. One thing. And you just can't! Do you even possess a brain?" Anita yelled into her burner phone. She pulled the ends of her hair in frustration, wanting to chuck the phone across the room. "Are you incapable of even the simplest thing? Did you even *book* my appointment yet?"

"Yes, I did! It's at five! And why can't you just do the resume yourself?" Tanya yelled back.

Anita's blood boiled. "Listen here, *thief.* You're going to do exactly as I say, and you're going to do it now. I want it sent to me in the next hour or things won't be looking so good for you." She cut the call and threw the phone behind her onto her bed. She sat down on the bed herself, and rubbed her hands. How could she have told Tanya the truth? How could she tell her that she hadn't had an education? She'd left school in early middle school and had never gone back. She could hardly write a page, let alone write a resume for herself.

Suddenly exhausted, she lay down on the bed, and let herself fall asleep.

✳✳✳

Her burner phone buzzed under her, waking Anita. She scrambled around for it, before grabbing it tightly. She picked it up, rubbing her eyes.

3:21

I'm done, how should I give it to you?

~t

Parking lot @ Carmen. Make sure no one sees you. Hide in the shadows.

She sat up and rubbed her eyes. Anita walked over to her closet and flung it wide open. She settled for a smart black pantsuit, over a white shirt, with black pumps. She quickly changed, and put her hair in a tight ponytail. She grabbed an empty briefcase from a drawer, and put a thick file in it. As she headed out, she looked at her watch. 3:45. Her phone began to buzz, her mother's name and number popped up. "Hello?" she said, unlocking her car.

"I'm at the hospital. I got hurt. "

"What?! How?!" she asked, panic rising up her throat.

"I was walking and then I fell. Can you come pick me up? I'm in All Saints Hospital," her mother said.

Anita calmed down, and put her hand on the steering wheel. "I'll be there in a half hour." She took a few deep breaths to calm herself down, before flying down the road, taking turns that could've landed her right next to her mother. She arrived at the hospital twenty-five minutes later and skidded into the emergency room.

Her mother was seated on one of the chairs, her injured leg resting on a small stool in front of her.

"Amma! Are you alright?" she asked.

Her mother smiled at Anita's concern, and waved her away. "I'm fine. Go sign me out," she replied.

Anita nodded, and walked towards the reception. "I'm paying the bill for Mrs. Chetana Javali," she said, taking out her wallet.

"Ma'am the bill has already been paid," the nurse said.

"What do you mean? By whom?"

"Vineeta Mishra," the nurse replied, referring to her computer.

Anita's heart stopped. She quickly thanked the nurse and rushed back to her mother.

"Why did someone else pay your bill Amma?" She tried her best to keep her voice steady.

Her mother's eyes lit up. "You'll never believe who it was! It's so funny because we were just talking about them! It was Maia's mother!"

"Yes, okay, great but why did she pay your bill?"

"Because she almost hit me with her car! I was crossing the road and didn't notice a car was coming until it was too late, she swerved and I fell, so she brought me here. How nice of her to pay the bill."

"Did she ask about me?" Anita asked.

Her mother chuckled. "You always wanted her approval. Yes, I mentioned you and she asked me how you were."

"Did you tell her anything about me?"

"No, how can I, when I know nothing?"

Anita huffed in relief. They left the hospital and Anita helped her mother to the car. Once behind the wheel, she remembered the job interview. She cursed under her breath, and hit the gas pedal.

"Why are you going so fast? Is there somewhere you have to be?" her mother inquired, holding the passenger assist handle tightly.

"Job interview," Anita muttered, not wanting her mother to press on the topic.

Her mother's face visibly brightened, as she fixed her eyes on the back of Anita's head. "Job interview?" She brought her hand down to her injured leg and leaned forward, so that her head was between the two front seats. "Where? What position?"

"Leave it Amma," she mumbled, her eyes on the road in front of her. She took a sharp left turn into a small alley, a few minutes later emerging on the large street where her house was located. "Get off here. I'll be back after some time."

"Okay. I suppose you can't tell me anything else about the interview?" her mother asked hopefully.

"Not a thing." Disheartened, Anita's mother hobbled out of the car and walked into the house, shutting the door tightly behind her.

Anita huffed in relief, and drove on. Her burner phone buzzed again, just as she stopped at a traffic signal.

4:53

Where are you?! People are starting to get suspicious!

Anita didn't bother to reply but sped along the road, creating a dust cloud for those behind her. She sped past small shops, and junkyards, smiling at how familiar those things were to her. She passed by screaming children, running as they slapped sticks against large tyres. Anita was struck by a sudden wave of nostalgia, and for a second imagined herself there, with those children, running without a care in the world. Their poverty didn't matter to them much, not yet. They were perfectly content with their tattered clothes and dirt-crusted skin.

Soon, larger buildings started to appear, morphing into skyscrapers. Her sleek black car fit into this background better, the car much more at home amongst fellow BMWs and Jaguars. In a matter of minutes, the large Carmen Industries building loomed in front of her, the largeness of the building casting a shadow over all the trees in front of it. Anita parked right outside and ducked out of her car. She walked past the security guards, hardly sparing them a look as they sat in a circle sipping on small cups of tea.

Anita ran her hand through her ponytail and looked around for Tanya. She spotted her; a tiny figure crouched against the dark shadows, eyes nervously flitting from side to side. Anita called her with a crooked finger.

Tanya stood up, straightening her clothes. She jogged towards Anita and passed it to her as she ran past.

Anita grabbed her hand and whispered in her ear: "Make sure I get out."

Tanya nodded without breaking her stride and continued running, before turning around a corner.

Anita leafed through the resume, soaking in the important points, before tucking the thick stack into her briefcase. She purposefully strode into the main building. A large desk took up one part of the large reception, the rest of the area arranged in groupings of sofas and chairs. A large skylight lit the whole office, with layers of balconies below it, all filled with people getting to work. She walked towards one of the receptionists and put her hand on the glass. "Hi, I'm here for a job interview," she said.

The woman looked up from her computer. "Your name?"

"Sareeka Kumar," she said, recalling the name that was written on her resume.

The woman nodded, her fingers gliding across the keyboard. "Yes, you can go up to the second floor, first door to your right. It's room 5. You shouldn't miss it, there's a large sign there that says 'Job Interviews'" The receptionist handed Anita a temporary access card and wished her luck.

Anita nodded her thanks with a smile. She waited for the elevator along with two women, who were engrossed in a discussion. She entered the elevator with them, and pressed 2.

"Yeah, his name's being dragged through mud right now. He has to really pick it up and give us directions if he wants to bring us back to the top," one of them said worriedly.

There was only one person they could be talking about. Garcia.

"Hmm. You're right. I would hate to lose my job right now, and I'm so close to a promotion," the other one replied.

The elevator doors slid open. Anita walked out, with a sidelong glance at the two women before the elevator doors shut again. She turned right, and immediately saw the large double doors, with a large brass number 5 on it and paper reading 'Job Interview.' Taking a deep breath, and running her plan through her mind once more, she pushed the door open. There was an elevated panel opposite a single desk, where five chairs were lined up. All of them were empty, except the one in the middle. And seated on it, was the person she needed to see most.

30

Mahesh Dube

"Richa, Richa, no listen to me. I need you to tell me the name of the person who just walked in," Dube said, waving his hands with frustration. He was pacing in his office, frantic.

"Sareeka Kumar. She's here for an interview. Sir, is there some sort of pr..."

"No, no! What room did you send her to?" he half-yelled.

"Room 5, second floor," the receptionist replied.

"Okay, I want you to tell all the people going down there to stop. I want to conduct this one myself. Is that understood?" he said, pressing the phone tightly to his ear.

"Yes sir, I'm on it," she said.

Dube hurriedly ran out of his office. He took the fire exit down to the second floor from his sixth-floor office and ran inside the interview room, panting. He seated himself on the chair, and took his phone out of his pocket. He scrolled through his contacts list, until he got to Garcia's contact. He requested for a video call, his leg jumping up and down in anticipation.

"What?" A voice snarled, sending a harsh vibration through Dube's phone. Dube jumped in fright and looked down at his phone. "You better have a good reason to call me. It's 8:30."

Dube rolled his eyes, and urgently said, "You have to see this. Remember that agent we hired to get that girl kidnapped?"

Garcia nodded.

"She's *here*. Under a fake name. For a job interview. I think she wants something."

"What would she want? She has her money."

"No. She wants something more. If it was just money, she wouldn't go this far. She would come straight up front. No, she wants something more. Much more."

The doors of the room opened. "Shhh, stay quiet and listen," Dube advised, and set his phone so that the whole room could be seen. A tall woman walked in. She glanced at the large panel for a second, before looking directly at Dube. She smiled. Dube's blood curdled, as he smiled back, and gestured for her to have a seat. Anita obliged and took a seat, placing her briefcase on the table.

Dube reached under his desk and took out a stack of papers. Anita's 'resume'. "So," he said. "Sareeka Kumar."

Anita raised an eyebrow before speaking. "Oh, come off it. Don't play dumb," she said. "You know exactly who I am, Mahesh."

Dube's breath hitched.

"Oh, and," Anita continued. "Hey Anthony," she said, blowing Dube's phone a kiss. "My assumption is that you are not very happy right now."

Dube snuck a glance at his phone, and indeed, Garcia's eyebrow was raised.

"Anyways," Anita settled into her chair. "I have a proposal."

"Proposal?" Garcia's voice cut through the silence.

"Yes. A proposal. Now, if you'll let me continue, we can actually get to the part of the day where you'll listen."

Dube beckoned for her to continue, his eyes tracking every movement. Anita clicked open her briefcase, and took out a file. Dube's heartbeat quickened. It was the same file that he and Garcia had given her.

"This is the file you gave me, when you asked me to kidnap Maia. Incidentally, both of your fingerprints are strewn across this whole thing. What more evidence do I need? And even then, you're only a phone call away from endless, endless courtrooms and eventually, a jail cell. So, here's the deal. You get Maia out and back safely to her parents in the next two days, or I'm afraid the police and federal agencies are a phone call away," Anita said, leaning forward across the table.

Suddenly a loud blaring noise erupted, startling both Dube and Anita. Dube looked around, before realizing it was coming from his phone. He looked into it. Garcia had an alarmed look on his face, and was holding up a piece of paper. *Get out*, it said, *we need to talk.* Dube stood up awkwardly, and cleared his throat.

"I'll be, um, back," he said, and walked towards the door.

"Take your time!" Anita called, leaning back in her chair.

Dube left the room.

"Lock the door, idiot," Garcia growled.

Dube nodded, hurried back to the door, and bolted it shut.

"So, what do we do?" Dube asked, scratching his jaw.

"This is completely and utterly unnecessary. She's just getting in the way. My plan was going along perfectly and now that little son of a- anyways, she needs to be taken care of."

"What- what do you mean? We can't *kill* her," he said in a low voice. "That may bring bad attention. We really cannot afford that right now. What I don't understand is why she's doing this. What's in it for her? I mean, she didn't even know Maia existed until a while ago!"

Garcia thought for a moment. "You're right. Killing is a bit messy. I think I have a better plan," he said. Before Dube could protest, he heard a click, as Garcia left him in the dark, once again.

✳✳✳

Dube unbolted the door of the interview room to be greeted with curtains billowing in the wind. Dube's heart raced.

She escaped.

He noticed a piece of paper fluttering on the table, and moved to pick it up.

You have a day to decide.

✳

Garcia

That betraying little, Garcia thought, as he slammed his fist on the table, driving his knuckles into the shiny redwood table. He could threaten to go to the police, but then again, he was a foreigner in this country, with no proof. He knew that if he talked to the authorities, so would she. And she had more on him at the moment. He knew that this was a possibility when he hired her, but he never thought she would to go through with it. What was he going to do? How would he stop her? Just as he was about to storm out of his hotel room, it hit him. Why, the solution was so simple. He would just take her as well.

31

Vineeta

"Madam?"

"Yes, Ramesh, quickly," Vineeta snapped, sitting up in bed.

"I was outside the Carmen Industries building. Tanya was there, and so was the other woman, what's her n-"

"Anita, yes, go on," she said urgently.

"Tanya had arrived at the building an hour or two before Anita did. She was hiding, I think, waiting in the shadows, until Anita came along. Then, she jogged past her and handed her a file. Anita slipped it into her briefcase and walked in. I wasn't able to follow her in. Tanya hung around the building, until Anita hurriedly left the building through a fire exit and both of them got into Anita's car. Tanya was dropped off at the school, and Anita went to her house, I think."

Vineeta exhaled. "Thank you, Ramesh. Keep me updated." She hung up, and lay back down on her bed.

Deep breaths. Deep breaths.

Her mind itched to call Dev, but she knew she couldn't. He was at a meeting, and couldn't be interrupted. Tears rolled down her cheeks, and she didn't bother to wipe them away. Even at a time like this, when their daughter was somewhere, in some corner, scared for her life, they had to continue working. They had to continue as if nothing had happened, like there was no problem at all. There was a timid knock on her door. It was her maid. "Ratna. I- do you need something?" she said, turning her head from the door towards the ceiling again.

"Ma'am," she said in Hindi. "I'm sure she's okay. Wherever she is, I'm sure she's okay." Her voice was tinged with worry.

"How can you be so sure?" Vineeta replied bitterly. She sat up in bed, and patted her tousled hair down.

"I just *know*. Wouldn't you feel it? As a mother? If something happened to her, wouldn't you know?" Ratna questioned, her black eyes piercing into Vineeta's brown.

Vineeta hung her head low. Would she? Seeing the type of mother she'd always been, would she know? "Yeah," she said, biting her lip, "I would know."

***

They sat at the long dinner table; platters of food left untouched. Vineeta pushed her food around with a fork, as Dev drummed the table.

"We should just go to bed. There's no point in staring at food we're not going to eat," Dev stated.

Vineeta nodded mutely and pushed her chair back.

Dev did the same, just as Vineeta's phone rang. "Who at this hour?" Dev questioned, as Vineeta picked up.

It was Ramesh. "Hello? Ma'am?!" he whispered, wind blowing behind him.

Vineeta pushed the phone closer to her ear, struggling to listen. "Yes, what's happened?"

"Somebody just broke into Anita's house! I left the school an hour ago, thinking there would be more action here. Two people suddenly appeared out of nowhere, and entered her house. They were dressed in black, and they're still there. Wa-wait one second, I think they're coming out and-" he gasped, and his voice became even more muffled.

Vineeta pressed the phone even closer and stole a quick glance at Dev, who was holding her elbow tightly. "Go on," she urged.

"Ma'am they're leaving, but they have something with them! I can't see what it i- oh my God, I think- I think that's a *body bag*."

Vineeta sucked in a breath. Her hands fumbled as she moved to put her phone on speaker.

"They're leaving in a car, I'm going to-" Ramesh stopped talking and they heard his footsteps at a run.

Dev looked at Vineeta, his eyes wide.

"Ma'am, the car has a Carmen Industries symbol on it. Should I follow it?"

"If it has a Carmen Industries symbol on it that means Garcia's behind this. And if Garcia's behind this, then there is a good chance that they're taking Anita to the same place they've kept Maia. I don't think Garcia would even bother to keep them apart," Dev said in a low voice. "Tell him to follow the car. And make sure he gets the number."

Vineeta told Ramesh to do the same, and cut the phone. She then pounded up the stairs, Dev hot on her trail.

"What are you doing?" he yelled behind her.

Vineeta ran into her room and grabbed her keys.

As she turned around, Dev grabbed her hands. "Vineeta, you can't," he protested.

"What do you mean I can't, this is our daughter we're talking about. I need to find that car. Do you even care?" Vineeta fought back, struggling to free herself from Dev's tight grasp.

But, as soon as the last four words left her mouth, Dev let go. His eyes widened with surprise and hurt, and he took a step back. Then, his eyes hardened. "What do you mean, I don't care? How could you even think that? This is our daughter you know? She's as much mine as she is yours. How dare you even say that to me? What has got into you? You need to see some *sense* Vineeta. You aren't going to find her by just following a car. Especially at this hour. I'm not- not caring. I'm just caring with caution," he said stonily, and walked away from the door, and back down the stairs.

Vineeta put her keys back on the nightstand. She knew she shouldn't have said it, but she couldn't help herself either. She just wanted to say something, something that would make someone else's feelings match hers. Her phone buzzed again, and she hastily picked it up.

"Ma'am, ma'am I lost the car." Ramesh said regretfully.

Vineeta put her head in her hands, and asked Ramesh where he lost the car.

"Near Electronic City, Ma'am," he said.

"Okay," she said, suddenly bone tired.

She lay down and tried to go to sleep. Not surprisingly, sleep didn't come.

Another day wasted.

32

Maia

Blood was pouring out of her back, each droplet falling onto a concrete road. There was a girl on the road, racing away on a bicycle. Maia ran behind her, and fell, twisting her ankle. A phone lay in front of her. The phone buzzed. You have one new notification, it said. She inched forward to pick it up, but suddenly she was in a forest, and rain fell, knocking trees over. A new laptop lay in front of an apartment, the keys in her hand. She unlocked the door, and walked in. There were several people inside, faceless. She walked towards one of them and tapped their shoulder. The person turned around. Maia reeled back with fear. The apartment dissolved, and everything turned black. A single sun emerged from the centre, and turned into eyes, the colour of hazelnuts.

Maia's eyes peeled open. She pushed her hair off of her sweaty forehead. She sat up, steadying herself with her hand. She could hear the blood pounding in her ears, her heart beating hard and fast under her skin.

Eyes, the colour of hazelnuts.

She shuddered, and took a deep breath. Her lower lip began to tremble, and before she knew it, tears were streaming down her cheeks.

All of a sudden, she heard a noise behind her. She froze, and slowly turned her head around. She gasped in fear, and crawled off the bed and crouched behind it, trying to forget her sprained ankle. Huddled in the far corner of the warehouse, was another figure, bound at the limbs by ropes. The person's head hung low, and occasionally bobbed in sleep. Raven black hair fell to the front, some strands touching the floor. A broken light flickered above her, casting long shadows on her face.

Maia stood up from her position behind her bed and reached for her shoes. She kept the spiky parts pointed outward, in hopes of using them as a weapon. She hobbled to where her fellow captor was bound and crouched in front of the woman. She prodded her in the arm. The woman raised her head with an effort, and their eyes met. Maia recoiled. It was her kidnapper. She crawled back, her eyes wide as saucers. As soon as she was beyond her reach, she stood up and wielded her shoes like a weapon. "You!" she said accusingly, pointing a trembling finger at the woman. "Wh-what are you doing here?" She tripped and staggered back, wincing. She put the shoe in front of her again, in an attempt to take control.

The woman's mouth was open, in an O. "Maia, Maia, you're alright!" she said, bringing her hands up, before realizing they were bound.

Maia brandished her shoe in the air. "What do you mean *I'm alright? You're half the reason I'm here! If it weren't for you, I bet, even Tan-"*

"Tanya brought it upon herself," the woman cut in harshly. She was trying to untie herself. "Why don't you untie me and we can talk?"

"Why would I help you, lady?" Maia asked.

"First, my name, is Anita. Second, I have no weapons on me."

"How can I be sure?"

"You think I wasn't frisked?"

Maia weighed her options. *There really is no way she could have any weapons, especially in those pants that hug her like a second skin.* She moved forward and inspected the knots. She pulled at the loose ends, but to no avail. "Freaking sailor knots," she muttered under her breath.

Try your medieval torture device of a shoe. It could probably kill someone," Anita remarked.

Maia. Calm down. You're rambling. And who knows? Maybe you'll have to kill someone? Maia shook her head and took her shoe. She hit the knots meekly, having no intention to help her fellow captive get free.

"Not like that, idiot. Aim the spikes," Anita said, exasperated.

"Oh... oh right." Maia replied.

After several long minutes, Anita was free. She stood up and stretched, moving her hands in circles. "Good. Now we need to get out of here," Anita said decidedly and moved towards the door.

"Hey, hey wait. Why did you want to know if I was okay? Why do you care?" Maia asked.

Anita stopped and turned around. "Don't you remember me?" she asked in a soft voice.

"Uh, no?" Maia replied.

"That scar, the one on your right arm, you still have it right?" Anita asked.

Maia subconsciously grazed her arm, right where the scar was. "How did you- you probably saw a picture or something," she said, straightening her arm.

"You were seven. You were climbing a tree, and then you fell off. You broke your arm. I was the one who called your parents at work."

"But no," Maia said, shaking her head. "That was with, I was with -with, oh my- *Annie?*"

Anita grinned. "The very same."

Maia's heart suddenly leapt up, before settling down again. How could she be sure? *Stupid, stupid, stupid. Shouldn't have untied her.* "I don't believe you," she mumbled.

Anita pursed her lips. "You don't have to, but we need to get out of here."

"Yeah, that's not so simple. I've tried, but there's literally no one that could open the gate from the outside. It is number locked from the outside. And it locks automatically once you shut it."

"No one. Are you sure?" Anita questioned, her hand on her chin.

"Yup. Just you and me. Well, you, me and Marie."

33

Anita

"Marie? Who's Marie?" Anita asked.

"The food lady," Maia replied with a shrug. She flung her shoes on a large straw bed and sat down on it. She pulled a scraggly blanket around herself. "She comes in pretty late at night, I think around three in the morning. I had this diamond bracelet that I gave her as a bribe. In return, she had to tell me why I was here." She looked at the floor.

Anita's heart softened, and she sat on the floor opposite Maia. "So, you know?"

"Well not really, she didn't actually provide me with any concrete information. But it is kind of stupid to bring me into this whole business though, don't you think? I mean, I know my parents just as much as some stranger on the street does."

Anita shifted awkwardly. "So," she said lightly. "About this Marie, is she trustworthy?"

"Yeah?" Maia said with uncertainty. "I don't know, I mean, I wouldn't bet on her loyalty, but yeah, she's pretty okay."

Anita closed her eyes in thought. "Okay, here's what," she said. "That lady..."

"Marie," Maia cut in.

"As soon as Marie comes in, I want you to immediately get the door. You have to keep it open, because it's not going to be easy to get the number from the lady, sorry, Marie. She's not going to give up the number easily." Anita stood up and paced the floor.

Maia watched her pace like a ball boy on a tennis court, with her back against the wall. "That's not going to be easy. She shuts it as soon as she comes in. There's no way I can stop the door and make sure she doesn't close it before," she said.

"And that's where I come in. I'm going to stand by the side and as soon as she comes in, hello roundhouse kick."

"Roundhouse kick. You know how to do a roundhouse kick?" Maia repeated.

Anita shrugged. They heard a low rumble from outside. A loud pitter-patter could be heard, beating against the metal ceiling. Anita groaned. "Really, really bad time," she muttered.

"So, what's your plan for after we get out? Do you even know where we are?"

"Yes. Yes, of course I do," Anita said, pointedly not looking at Maia.

"Ah yes," Maia said, nodding. "And where are we, exactly?"

"Um...a forest?"

"Nice work, Detective"

Anita chuckled softly. "It's funny isn't it? That we had to meet after all these years, like this?"

Maia leaned forward again, a serious look on her face. "Can I ask you something?"

"Go ahead," Anita replied warily.

"Why am I here? I mean, I know it's probably because of my parents, but what's the real reason?"

"I'm not completely sure, but here's what I was able to find out," Anita said and told Maia about the articles she had read, and the men she had met.

"And what about you?" she asked.

"What about me?" Anita asked, surprised, although she had a faint idea as to what Maia was going to say.

"Why do you do this? This whole criminal thing?"

✳✳✳

It was one of the worst monsoons Anita had ever experienced. The rain was falling hard and fast, soaking her from head to toe. She ran into her house, let the water rivulets drip onto the thin mat. She could hear her parents yelling from inside the house.

"What do you mean you're too sick to work? Who's going to bring in the money now hmm?" Her mother's harsh words cut through the air like a knife, each word thrown out, dangling into the air.

"You bring in enough! I can hardly speak, yet alone move!" Her father's voice was raspy and thin. "I don't have any energy left in me anymore! I can't do this anymore!"

"You can't do this anymore? You can't do this anymore? All you do is stand around, flipping dosas all day! I have a child to take care of, so many houses to work in!"

"Is that what you think? If you think your job is so high and mighty, then why do you need me to do anything? Just go do all the work by yourself. I am absolutely sick of you. Sick of you and all your drama. I can't take this. The second I'm better, assuming I get better, I'm leaving. I'm leaving you. I'm leaving everything to do with you."

Anita couldn't breathe for a second. She slipped back out of her house, and ran down the street. The heavy rain had dwindled down to a slight drizzle now, but the streets were still empty. She continued to run until she couldn't anymore, fighting back her tears.

She stopped after what felt like hours, panting with her hands on her knees. She looked around, and saw large houses and expensive cars lining the streets. She had no idea where she was. She sat with her knees on the ground and covered her eyes. She let the tears fall. She let them fall onto the wet ground, let them cloud her vision. She cried until she could cry no more, until she felt like all her body was drained of water and was completely hollow. She wiped her eyes and stood up.

The largest visible house was in front of her, an Italian-style mansion sprawled across prime real estate. Her body suddenly started to work faster than her mind, her legs pulling their way to the large front gates. She climbed over them without a second thought and jumped onto the soft, wet freshly-mown grass. She sprinted across the front yard and stopped in front of a large window. The lights were turned on inside, the curtains pulled back. She pushed the window slightly, and felt it give way. She climbed inside and looked around the room with wide eyes.

It was the most beautifully decorated thing she had ever seen, the yellow light swathing room with a warm glow. Plush seats lined a long dining table, buffet tables bordered the sides of the room. Bronze candelabras were placed across the whole room, along with other trinkets that made it look timeless yet modern at the same time. Anita stroked one of the candelabras, just as she heard a sound from inside the house.

"Who's there?" she heard a voice call.

Her muscles seized for a second. Anita picked up one of the candelabras and darted to the window.

"Oi! Oi! Who are you? Stop right there, I'm calling the police!" The voice said, now almost directly behind her.

Anita stole a quick glance behind her. A man in his late forties stood in front of her with stormy eyes. He was wearing a dark red robe with golden designs on it. He was making his way towards her, a phone in one hand, a cricket bat in the other. A cool breeze of wind blew behind her, loudly shutting the window. Her blood ran cold. She moved backwards, hitting a wall. Her legs were trembling. "Please," she whispered, her hands clammy. "Please let me go." She pushed the back of the window again, but it refused to budge.

The man's eyes flashed and he raised the bat high above his head.

At that exact moment, almost on an impulse, Anita flung the candelabra she was holding at the man. It hit him straight in the forehead, knocking him to the ground.

Without further ado, she ran past the man's prostrate body and into the main room. She didn't have time to admire its beauty. She frantically looked around for the main door. She ran down the single corridor opposite the grand staircase, and pulled open the door. It was a bedroom. Her chest tightened as she ran out of the room and opened every other door she could find. Fifteen doors later, she pulled open the front door. She was greeted by a blast of cold air, as she ran out onto the front yard.

She ran, moving as fast as her legs could take her, back to her rundown neighbourhood, back to the rundown houses with broken windows and asbestos sheets. She skidded into her house, and put her back against the wall, panting. The house was silent as she walked to the only bathroom in the house and splashed her face with ice-cold water. She unlocked the door, and saw her father.

"Appa," she said, her voice trailing off as she looked at his frail body. She then suddenly hugged him tight, and buried her head in his chest.

Her father hugged her back uncertainly, as Anita cried into his kurta. "Anita, what happened?" he asked gently.

Anita shook her head and continued to cry.

At that moment, her mother walked in. "What's happening here?" she screeched. "Anita, why are you crying? What's wrong with you? You're sixteen years old. Grow up!"

Anita pulled away from her father reluctantly, and walked past him, and lay on her straw bed. She slept fitfully that night, dreaming of candelabras and dark, dark red.

The next day, her father went to work. Anita woke up late in the afternoon to an empty house. She wandered outside, before heading to her father's dosa stall. It was crowded and her father looked absolutely worn out. He was sitting on a plastic chair and flipping dosas, the bags under his eyes prominent. Anita's heart went out to him, as she ran up to the stall and began to help him. She was rewarded with a pleased smile and several more orders. Just as she flipped what felt like her hundredth dosa, she heard something that made her heart stop beating.

"Did you hear what happened last night?" a man said conversationally as he snacked on a paper dosa.

"No, what happened?" the man next to him asked.

"You know that big house a little way out of this area? The one with the big gates and garden? The owner was murdered last night."

No, no. It wasn't me. I didn't do that.

"What? How did he die? I was his driver five years ago!" the other man said, in horror.

"He was hit with something. The papers said it was something metal. The police think with a candle holder."

Anita looked down pointedly, her hands and legs shaking uncontrollably. I didn't kill him. I didn't kill him.

"Anita, are you okay? You just burnt that dosa." Her father's voice cut in.

I didn't kill him. I didn't kill him. *She mumbled an apology and dumped it, starting over. Her father's eyes bore into her, going past her body into her soul. Oh God, I killed him. She wondered if he was seeing her the way she was looking at herself. Like a murderer.*

Two months after that, her father left home, cured and healthy. He left Anita and her mother in the middle of the night, no note, no letter. Although she hadn't told anyone, Anita was sure her father knew she had done it. It was the way he looked at her, and the way he stopped speaking to her before he left.

Anita got over it eventually, and no one knew her secret. At least that's what she thought.

Thirteen months later, she got a letter in the mail. The letter said the sender knew she had killed someone, and was willing to reward her handsomely if she did it again. To a different person.

Two weeks later, a woman lay dead in her 17th floor apartment, a knife in her side and a suicide note clutched tightly in her hand.

No one ever suspected it was murder.

✳✳✳

"Earth to Anita." A hand was waving around Anita's face.

Anita closed her eyes to clear her head. "Sorry, yeah, what did you ask me?"

"I asked you why you're doing this," Maia moved her hand, as if to express what exactly Anita was doing. "Why you're being a - a criminal."

"Pays well," Anita replied shortly, not meeting Maia's eyes.

"Fine," Maia muttered. A boom sounded all around the shed, making both of them start forward. The light swayed dangerously. Maia's eyes widened. "Don't tell me. You're scared of lightning. Are you kidding?"

Anita shrugged. "Don't blame me, what can I do? I've been scared since I was little. And hey, I didn't see you cruise through that either."

"I was startled. Not *afraid*. And can't we wait until tomorrow? There are a lot of bad things that can happen during lightning - for example, death."

"No. There's no point. There isn't much time."

Maia pulled her blanket closer. "It's getting chilly. Hey, what's today's date?"

"December 28th. Why?"

Maia muttered to herself before shaking her head. "Remember my dollhouse?"

"How could I forget?" Anita replied fondly, remembering the walk-in house Maia had as a child. They would spend hours inside, pretending to be grown up. They would drink water in teacups and hold faux meetings. "I don't think it qualified as a dollhouse actually, it was more of a *human* house."

Maia chuckled at this.

"You know," Anita began. "You didn't seem too surprised or scared when I said you didn't have much time."

Maia shrugged. "I don't know, I kind of always figured this would happen someday or the other, you know? Maybe not kidnap. But definitely something - something bad. It was waiting to happen," she said, biting her lip.

The rain was falling harder than ever, making it hard to hear what Maia was saying. Anita moved closer to the bed, as Maia rubbed her eyes.

"It's getting late. Do you have a watch, by any chance?"

Anita nodded and looked at her left arm. "It's-it's gone," she said with surprise.

"What do you reckon the time is?" Maia asked.

Anita scooted over to one of the boarded-up windows and peeped outside through one of the slits. Cold air whispered outside, and the night sky was darker than any blue she had ever noticed. Trees obscured her vision, shooting up from the ground into tall, dark silhouettes against the sky. "I'd say it's pretty late –well past midnight."

Maia smiled half-heartedly. "That's good. That means we don't have to wait for much longer. She should be here."

In reply, Anita stood up and walked over to the large gates and positioned herself beside them, ready to pounce on anyone who walked through them. "You should probably break your heels off of your shoes - there's no way you can run barefoot in the rain or with those heels."

Maia's expression clouded over as she looked over at her shoes. She stroked them lovingly before abruptly snapping off the heels.

"Keep the heels. You may need them. Chuck me one, actually," Anita said.

Maia threw Anita a heel, just as a loud screech was heard from outside. Maia squeaked and threw herself on the bed, pushing the covers over herself.

Anita steadied herself, just as the gate groaned open. The tray came first, followed by a plump set of hands. As soon as she spotted elbows, Anita pounced. As she flew through the air, she saw the tray suddenly bolt forward. She collided with the woman in the air, and rolled onto the floor, tackling the woman trying to get away on top of her. Anita kicked out, rolling over so she was on top of the woman. As soon as she could steady herself, she brought her fist backwards and slammed it as hard as she could into the woman's face. The woman yelled in pain, her features twisting before smoothing out completely. Anita stood up and brushed off her clothes as if to get rid of some invisible dust.

"Is she... dead?" Maia said after a long pause.

Anita looked up and surprise and saw Maia standing at the gates, holding it open with all her strength, just a sliver, so that nobody on the outside would notice. "No," Anita said. "Maybe. Doesn't matter. Come on, we need to get out of here. Give me your hand."

Maia slipped her hand into Anita's, holding it tight. "Whatever you do, do not let go."

Both of them pushed the door open and were met with a spray of rain and cold air.

34

Vineeta

Vineeta and Dev sat opposite each other awkwardly, separated by a vast array of breakfast foods on the table.

"Sorry," Vineeta muttered under her breath, pushing soggy cornflakes around the bowl with her spoon.

"What?" Dev asked, looking up.

"I'm sorry," Vineeta repeated, clearing her throat.

Dev set his spoon down with a clatter, and sighed. "I don't need a sorry, Vineeta. I need you to understand. We need to get her back, and panicking and shutting everyone out isn't going to do that. We need to do something about it. We don't have much time. Nothing's going to happen if there's a huge wall between us."

Vineeta nodded into her bowl. She knew he was right. "What should we do then?"

"I think there is only one thing we can do."

Vineeta gulped.

✳✳✳

Vineeta's phone buzzed. She knew exactly who it was. She clicked on it, her finger trembling.

"I'm an impatient man, so I've decided to cut your time short. You want your daughter; I want your company. Bring the papers to the New Fresh Café near the Suvarnamukhi forest and you'll get your daughter back in one piece." The phone clicked, signifying the call was over.

Vineeta dropped her phone onto the polished wood floor, her hands shaking uncontrollably as she bent down to retrieve it.

Dev was staring at her dumbfounded, before he put his phone to his ear in a hurry. "Suvarnamukhi forest, Suvarnamukhi forest. Vinny, that's a good 25 to 30 kilometres away. We have to leave immediately. We have

148

to negotiate a sale price. It doesn't matter, he can have it for how much ever," he muttered pacing up and down the corridor.

"But - but, we can't just *hand the company over*," Vineeta said, tugging at the ends of her hair.

Dev slowly turned around and looked at her. His face flipped through several emotions, before settling on one. "He has our daughter Vineeta!" he roared. "Stop thinking about the company for once and think about your daughter! Your family! Get your priorities straight. One second all you care about is your daughter, and once the opportunity to get her back shows up all you care about is the company! Companies and names can be brought back once they're gone! Our daughter cannot."

Vineeta shrank into the wall, flinching at his sharp words as they pierced her soul.

*

Dev

Pathetic.

A great example of a word he never thought he'd use to describe his wife. His hands and body tingled with rage and confusion, and his head spun. He couldn't even look at her, even glance at her because all he could see was his family falling apart. Their daughter was gone, and now, so were they.

His legs moved by themselves, out of the living room, past the dining room, and through a small door so red in colour it almost looked as if it was a part of the royal red wall. He pushed it open, and turned the light on. Dim white light flooded the small room, bringing out spooky shadows in the middle of the morning. The room was empty, save the large metal locker that took most of the wall adjacent to the door.

Taking a deep breath, Dev punched in a number *1307*. 13th July. Her birthday.

He pulled the heavy metal door open, and stepped inside. The room was lined with shelves, all important documents pertaining to the company. He picked a few of them and left the room, shutting the doors tight behind him. As he stepped back into the main part of his house, he squinted his eyes, trying to adjust his eyes to the sudden light. When he went back to the living room, his wife wasn't there.

✳✳✳

He drove in silence, his eyes glued on the road. He drove straight ahead, his heart beating faster than the car was moving. Thunder rumbled overhead, grey clouds crowding the dull blue evening sky.

"I'm sorry," Vineeta whispered, her head out the window.

"Funny how when you say a word so many times it loses its meaning," Dev said sharply.

Vineeta pushed her messy hair away from her face. "I'm trying - I really am. But I'm just so- so confused for some reason. Obviously, Maia is my - our number one priority, but this company is just as much our child. I couldn't bear to part with either."

Dev hit the accelerator, as the car whizzed by village after village. Small droplets of water started to fall, hitting the windshield and rolling down. Dev bit his lip. He didn't know what to say. What did she want him to say? What would he tell her? That it was okay to even for a second consider giving up your daughter for a job?

"I understand if you have nothing to say to me. I wouldn't either, if I were you. I've been trying to understand it. But I can't. And I didn't expect it to be like this."

He looked at Vineeta briefly, and saw a single tear streak down her cheek. He looked away with a sigh. He didn't know how to reply. He didn't want to. The rain fell hard and fast now, drowning the deafening silence in the car.

"The café. I see it," Vineeta said ten minutes later, as a small dingy café came into view.

New Fresh Café it read.

✳✳✳

The café was old and musty, with no people inside. At the sound of the door opening, an old man emerged from behind a door, but at Dev's command retreated into his hideout. Dev and Vineeta stood, looking around, unsure of what they were supposed to do.

"Let's sit," Dev said, breaking the pregnant silence in the room. They took a seat and waited for their daughter's fate to be decided.

✳

Dube

"You want me to go alone?" Dube asked incredulously.

"Yes. I will come after some time. I have another matter to tend to."

Dube looked at him suspiciously. "Well, can I have my phone back at least? You've had it for over four days."

Garcia nodded and retrieved Dube's phone from his back pocket. "Well, be on your way then. You know what you have to do. Try not to disappoint me."

Dube huffed in frustration. He mentally prepared himself for the meeting, and to battle some old demons.

Two hours later, the cafe came into view. Dube's heart started beating fast, as he stepped out. On any other day the décor of the café coupled with the raging storm would have scared Dube. But now, what lay inside, scared him so much more.

✳✳✳

"You think if we dress like them, we can be like them?" Mahesh's friend Rahul whispered into his ear, as they passed by a large group of boys, huddled around each other, all laughing and thumping each other on the back. While they were dressed much like everyone else, it was the subtle hints that gave it away; the way their shirts just fit them better, or how their clothes always looked brighter against the sun than theirs did. Most of them were incredibly rich, and didn't care about their education anymore. They would all inherit their fathers' businesses one day.

Mahesh looked at Rahul with narrowed eyes. "Why does it matter? We're in college, who cares about popularity?" he said. You do, a voice inside him hummed. While Mahesh tried not to care about who was important and who was not, it constantly piqued him that he was included in the 'not' category. When he left for college, everything was supposed to have changed. When he had taken off his school bag for the last time, he had simultaneously taken off the person he used to be.

One semester into his first year, and he was already turning back into his old self. As they walked to class, he eyed the central axis of the group, a handsome second year student named Dev Mishra. While he was the epitome of popularity, his grades were consistently perfect, never once faltering. If this wasn't enough to make someone envy him, there was also the matter of him being richer than most people combined. But he was different from the rest, always a touch nicer, and an incredibly hard worker. With a shake of his head, Mahesh pulled Rahul away from them.

"It's not worth the fight anyways. Once we get out of here, we'll show them who's the real boss." Mahesh said with false confidence.

"We will? Rahul said.

Mahesh nodded, more to convince himself. "Of course. Just you wait, in ten years, we'll be swimming in money, and they'll still be struggling to get jobs. I'm sure of it." With every word Mahesh said, he prayed. He prayed that for once, the stars would align in his favour, and grant him a wish.

✳✳✳

It was 2 a.m. and Mahesh was the only first year student awake, studying. There were books spread out all over his bed and floor, and he flitted from one book to another, like a moth attracted to light. Everyone else was at a party and Mahesh was perfectly content being alone. Mahesh went to the window and looked out. The wind was cool against his face.

"Mahesh! Mahesh! Come down here. I need help." He heard a voice whisper from below him. He looked down, and to his surprise, Dev Mishra standing in the entryway of his hostel.

"Yes bhaiyya?" he called, leaning forward.

"I need help with a math problem," Dev said. He seemed to be drunk, but

Mahesh felt excited nonetheless. A second-year student was asking him, a measly first year student for help? His friends would never believe him.

"One second bhaiyya, I'm coming!" Mahesh ran down the stairs as fast as his legs could take him. "What's the problem?" he asked.

"My book isn't here. We're all studying on the roof. Come with me," Dev said.

"We?" Mahesh asked. Dev Mishra's friends scared Mahesh. They would always bully him, and say rude things. Dev was a lot nicer, even though he occasionally participated.

"Oh, you know, the others."

"Okay," Mahesh gulped. "Let's go."

They climbed all the way up to the roof of the hostel, past the sixth floor. Dev banged the door open. Immediately Mahesh realised something was wrong. What he saw was no study session. Empty glass bottles lay scattered all around the floor, and five of Dev's friends sat on overturned plastic crates, smoking. "Oho, look who came back! That too with our favourite junior!" one of them slurred. Two of them walked towards Mahesh, as he tried to back away. "Arre, where are you going? Come, come, maths doubt is there, na?" they said, and began to laugh. They brought him to the middle of their circle, as Mahesh gave Dev a frightened look.

"Guys, wait," Dev started, but it was too late. Mahesh felt a sharp pain against his jaw, and fell to the floor.

"Wait, stop!" he screamed, putting his hands in front of him. But it was too late. The pain spread to all parts of his body like fire, as each boy took his turn, beating him senseless. Right before Mahesh lost consciousness, he turned to his side and said to Dev as loud as he could. "I trusted you."

✷✷✷

Mahesh was found the next morning, lying in the middle of a clean roof, the bottles and cigarettes long gone, with the limp body with the horribly crooked leg being the only testament to the soiree that had taken place the night before.

✷✷✷

Dube took a deep breath and pushed the door open. Instantly, the only two people inside looked at him and stood up. He mustered up as much confidence as he could and looked them straight in the eyes, with a smirk on his face. The man recognised him instantly, and his eyes changed for a second before they dimmed again.

I hope you've experienced the same pain. Mahesh said to him mentally, as he took a seat.

"Well, let's get started; shall we?"

*

Tanya

Tanya was pacing in her room, her mind thinking fifty different things at once. Anita hadn't contacted her since the interview was supposed to have happened, and she had no clue where she was now. The burner phone no longer worked. Tanya was clueless. As the days had passed by, Tanya's guilt had begun to intensify, until she felt solely responsible for everything. *You're not wrong you know.* A tiny voice in the corner of her mind nagged, threatening to send her into a downward spiral.

I have to do something. There has to be something that I can do to help her.

In the back of her mind, Tanya knew there was only one thing that could be done. With trembling hands, she picked up her phone, and took a deep breath.

*

Mahesh

Mahesh heard police sirens. He heard them all around him, as the police stormed into the tiny cafe. Four police officers pointed their guns at Mahesh.

"You are under arrest for the kidnap of Maia Mishra," one of the officers said as Mahesh stood up, his hands in the air.

"No, wait! This is a misunderstanding! I'm innocent, I'm a placeholder for Anthony Garcia! This was his plan!" Mahesh yelled, as the couple were rushed out by the remaining officers.

"Please come with us to the police car, or we will be forced to handcuff you," another officer said, as Mahesh put his head in his hands.

"No, no, it wasn't me!" he said, but moved towards the car. He had to contact Garcia. He wouldn't go down for this. He wouldn't.

Epilogue

2 weeks later

Maia

When twelve medical examinations, four doctors and a trip to London still kept Maia mute, her parents finally decided to get her a therapist. One of her doctors suggested a music therapist, to help her engage and ease off her PTSD. That Saturday, Maia found herself seated in front of the liveliest woman she had ever met.

"Okay, so what's your instrument of choice?" Avantika asked, as she strummed a chord on her guitar.

Maia didn't move.

"Well, we'll just start with the guitar then?" she said brightly, as she continued to strum her guitar. She hummed a tune, words spilling out of her mouth.

Maia continued to stare blankly at the wall, the music hardly registering.

Avantika came over every day, and brought a different instrument. The day of their eighth session, Avantika walked in with bongos around her neck, and a tambourine in her hand. "Today, we're letting our anger out! Every time we hit this drum, we'll be expelling our worries and fears into the atmosphere where we will never see them again!" She pranced into the room and set the bongos in front of Maia.

"You drum, I'll tambourine. Let's go!" Avantika started hitting the tambourine against her palm, the jingle of it resonating around the room.

Suddenly, Maia was drawn to the drums, wanted to hit it until she knocked it senseless. She picked them up, unsteady of their weight and hit one softly. There was a hollow sound, and she wasn't sure if it was just Avantika's words getting to her, but she could almost swear she saw a puff come out of the drum. She hit it again, then continued to bang it harder and harder.

Avantika played along with the tambourine and within a minute, they had a steady beat going.

Maia began to enjoy it and let out a little giggle.

"That's right! Let's laugh it out!" Avantika forced a laugh as well, until they were both laughing for no reason at all. For the first time since she had been back, the tears that left her eyes were filled with something other than despair.

"Okay! Do you want to switch?" Avantika asked, as she handed the tambourine to Maia. Maia took it and began to hit it against her palm. Almost as if the sky was listening, there was a clap of thunder outside. Instantly, Maia's thoughts began to spiral, jumbling over one another. She began to see spots, as parts of the room blacked out.

Branches came flying towards her, scratching her face and legs. She ran faster, her dead feet sinking into the slushy forest floor as Anita led the way, her hand clasped tight around Maia's. She could hear the burly guards running behind them, their loud and hard words cutting through the vengeful nature of the incensed sky.

"We have to move quicker," Maia yelled to Anita. "They're catching up to us!"

Anita nodded, and tried to move her legs faster on the wet mud. They ran for another hundred metres, when Maia heard a loud sound, from right behind her. In an instant, the hand she was holding lost its grip, and Anita fell to the ground. Maia's heart clamped with fear, as she turned around to face the worst. Anita lay sideways on the floor, clutching her shoulder. She let out a tortured shriek. Maia gasped and looked up. They were catching up. Maia slipped into the thick hide of trees, dragging Anita's unconscious body as best as she could. She hid them between two trees, and carefully waited for the men to pass by. Her ankle felt like it was on fire, but she did her best to ignore it.

"Anita, Anita, wake up. Wake up!" Maia pleaded, shaking Anita's prostate body. Anita's eyes fluttered for a second, and went still again. "No, no, no, please, wake up!" she cried. Desperate tears rolled her cheeks, mixing with the raindrops that still kept falling steadily.

"Go," she heard Anita say softly. "Save yourself."

"I can't! I can't just leave you here!" Maia cried hysterically.

"Come back if you can," Anita said, laying her head down the forest floor.

Maia squeezed her hand one last time, and ran away.

"Maia, Maia, it's okay," she heard Avantika's voice over the sound of the pounding in her head.

Tears streamed down her cheeks as she whimpered and buried herself under her sheets. "Go away, just go away, please," she begged, pulling her quilt tighter around her. Her most comfortable pyjamas suddenly felt like cardboard against her skin. She felt Avantika's weight leave the bed, but she knew she was still there.

Suddenly, she heard the strum of a guitar, and Avantika started singing. It was a French song, but Maia wasn't listening hard enough to understand. The tears eventually stopped, but Maia remained under the covers, Avantika's song enveloped her like another blanket, to shelter her from the darkness that lay just outside her window.

✳✳✳

"Mumma!" Maia saw her mother at the edge of the forest, the light from her car casting an eerie glow on her silhouette.

"Maia?!" her mother yelled into the darkness.

"Mumma!" Maia limped into her mother's arms, her tears mixing with the rain. She saw police officers a little distance away, coming towards her. "Mumma, we have to find her! She's in there!"

Her mother looked at her. "Who? Who's in there? Come, we have to get you out of the rain, you're going to get sick." Her mother's voice trembled.

"Anita! She got shot, she's going to die!" Maia sobbed, as one of the police officers wrapped a blanket around her shoulders. "You have to go! Please! We have to save her!"

"Maia, honey, what are you talking about?" Vineeta said gently, rubbing Maia's shoulders.

Maia swatted them away and glared at her mother. "No! We have to save her!" She began to flail her arms, until Vineeta went over and spoke to a police officer. They immediately ran into the woods, their torches slicing through the darkness.

The rain had reduced to a light drizzle. Vineeta hugged Maia again, holding on for what felt like forever. "Oh, I'm so glad you're safe. I'm never going to let you out of my sight again."

"Where's Dad?" Maia asked.

Vineeta pulled Maia's blanket tighter around her shoulders. "He's just dealing with some things. He'll be here soon."

"Can we go home?" Maia asked, her voice breaking.

Vineeta looked at her with tears in her eyes.

"Soon," she said.

✳✳✳

"I want to go see Anita. I have to see her. I need to know she's okay," Maia said to her mother, pulling her robe tighter around herself.

Vineeta looked up from her newspaper. She had a look in her eyes that Maia couldn't recognise. She folded the paper and kept it on the side table. "I think you should sit down," Vineeta said, gesturing uncertainly to the armchair opposite her.

"Why? What happened to her?!" Maia asked, a sense of urgency creeping into her voice, as she took a seat.

"You can't see Anita," Vineeta started as Maia began to cut in. "Let me finish. You can't see her, because she's not here anymore."

"What do you mean she's not here?" Maia said, panicking. "Did she move away?"

Vineeta huffed in relief. "Yes, they transported her to a hospital in the US, for her treatment," Vineeta said.

"Oh," Maia said deflated. "We'll see her when she gets back right?"

"Yes, of course," Vineeta replied, and picked up the newspaper again. As she hid her face behind it, Maia stood up and walked away, wondering about the odd look in her mother's eyes.

***

"Maia."

Maia pulled the covers from over her head and peered out. Her father stood at the door, the night darkening his silhouette.

"Dad, what's wrong?" she asked, her speech laced with sleep.

"Nothing, I- you can go back to sleep," he said, shaking his head.

"No, tell me. What happened?" she asked, sitting up.

"I just had to see if you were okay," he said, his voice breaking.

"Of course, I'm fine!" she said, before softening her voice. "Dad, nothing's going to happen again. Everything's okay. We're all fine and that's the important thing."

Her father shook his head, and sat on the edge of her bed. "I should be the one saying these things to you.

"Who cares?" Maia said. "You need to stop worrying about whether it was your fault. It wasn't. It wasn't anyone's fault but that maniac's. And it's a pity we've decided to stay quiet about the truth to protect ourselves."

"It's better in the long run. Trust me, we don't need a man like that out to get us. He thinks he's won. But you can't really be the winner if it's based on a lie, right? That man will pay his dues someday. Someday just doesn't happen to be today. For now, we focus on you. You and only you," her father said.

"What about the company?" Maia asked. Her parents had been home since she got back. The question had been nagging at her in the back of her mind, but she didn't have the nerve to ask herself if she really wanted to know the answer.

"The company is not our priority right now. You are. We made the mistake of putting our work before our own child, and we don't plan to ever do it again. It shouldn't have happened in the first place," her father said.

"What are you going to do with it though, Papa?"

"We're selling. Go back to bed. It's late. Goodnight." He pulled the covers back over her and walked towards the door.

"Dad?" Maia called. He turned around, and Maia was transported back to all the nights when she was younger, her mind racked with nightmares as her father calmed her down.

"Yes?" he asked.

"Thanks," she said, smiling. Her father nodded once, and walked away, as the dark returned.

*

Tanya

There was a knock on her door. The knob turned as a woman entered the room. She had large and piercing brown eyes, with lustrous chestnut brown hair that cascaded down her shoulders in loose ringlets. She was full figured and was dressed in a hoodie and jeans, with a tote bag slung over her shoulder. She strutted into the room and sat on a chair purposefully. Tanya watched her, her arms crossed across her chest, the highest form of defiance she could think of at the moment.

"Welcome, to Richmond Youth Camp. I'm Aaryahi, commonly known as Lali, and I'm going to be your mentor for the duration of your stay," Lali said, as she extracted a notepad from her bag. "Now, you're going to be here for our eighteen-month program. I understand that you turn eighteen soon, which means that by the time you're ready to be a competent and responsible citizen again, you'll be nineteen. You will be required to attend some pre-college courses provided by teachers within the organization. My job is to help you understand and analyse your behaviour, and hopefully change it for the better. Once we understand your behaviour, we work towards finding your strengths and developing them into new skills. We'll be looking into ways to cure your kleptomania and also work on a number of social and moral skills. Over time, we'll also start building your college application. So, what are your interests?"

Tanya looked at her squarely in her face. "To get out of here, I don't belong here. I don't need to be here, I'm perfectly fine." She stood up, and walked to the window by her bed.

She was in a dormitory, a large square room with warm yellow walls. She was sharing it with three other girls, each of whom had their own bed, with a small bedside table and a cupboard. Tanya hadn't brought anything with her, because she knew she wasn't meant to stay. But there was something in Lali's voice, a finality that Tanya couldn't tolerate.

Lali looked at her. "Stage one, denial," she said, writing some notes on her notepad.

"What?" Tanya snapped.

"The five stages of grief: denial, anger, bargaining, depression and acceptance. Look, I know you don't want to be here. No one wants to be in a Juvenile Detention Centre. You're lucky that this is one of the better places. Your parents made sure of that. But you're here because something happened that the police got to know about, and we have to fix that. It's going to be hard, but in the end, it's going to be worth it. I've worked here for eight years, and there hasn't been one single relapse. And you aren't going to be our first."

Tanya turned around to face Lali. "That sounds like a great speech. I'm impressed. Now if you could just show me the way out, university starts in a month," Tanya said flatly, making her way to the door.

"No university will take you now. There's a permanent mark on your record, and until you can prove that you're not a threat, you will always be treated like one out there. What you did was very serious Tanya, and we need to ensure that it doesn't happen again," Lali said quietly.

Tanya stopped. She hadn't thought of that. But surely, she had never been a threat, had she? She had just done what she was told, in order to protect herself. Hadn't she? "You're lying. There's nothing wrong with me. I'm the one that told the police, you know. I called Ramesh and I made him call the police. Stop lying! I don't need to be here," Tanya said.

"I'm not. Ask any of the other girls around here. The girls you're sharing with? One of them has been charged as an accessory to murder, and she's only fourteen. The other? She was charged with having knowingly accepted stolen property from someone else. The someone else is her uncle, and he's got off scot-free, even though he stole. You may have been born with seven silver spoons in your mouth, but that doesn't mean they can't fall out. We'll start your sessions tomorrow," Lali said and stood up to leave.

"Wait," Tanya said. "Do I get to have any visitors?"

"Once a week with a supervised family outing once a month." With that, Lali left Tanya alone; in an empty room so charged with shattered dreams that Tanya couldn't help but feel suffocated by the fantasies that had once been hers.

*

Garcia

"Sir! Sir! What does this mean for the company?"

"Will rankings continue to fall?"

"Does a stunt like this harm your contracts with clients?"

"What is your opinion on the recent events?"

"Don't answer them, they'll twist your words and make you look like the devil," Garcia's PR said, pushing through the throng of people waiting outside the office.

"No, I need to tell them," Garcia said. He stopped in front of a reporter with a microphone in his hand. "Good evening. My name is Anthony Garcia. I have to tell you the truth, once and for all."

Instantly, he heard pin-drop silence.

"Yes, I knew there was a company that had overtaken us in India. Yes, I knew that I wanted to get back to the top. But that was only through hard work. I never had any criminal intentions. When I hired Mahesh Dube a few years ago, and gave him such a high-ranking position, it was because I saw calibre in him. I thought he was a hard worker. But, and very unfortunately I was wrong. He came to me, and told me about a master plan he had to kidnap the poor girl to distract the parents. I flat out said no, because I have always been against crime. If you lose something, you work to get it back, not take a shortcut. I'm glad Mahesh Dube is in jail, away from society, where he will not pose a threat to anyone. Especially not my company. Thank you." Garcia walked away, straightening his suit, as a hundred cameras flashed behind him. His PR followed, yelling, "No further comment!" as questions flew through the air.

"Sir, your flight to Brazil is in three hours, is there anywhere else you would like to go before this?" his PA asked, whipping out his phone.

"Back to the office. I need to wipe out all traces of that criminal from my office," Garcia said, climbing into the car that stood in front of him. "But first, let's go to prison."

"Sir?!" his PA asked.

"To see Mahesh Dube, you imbecile. Take me there," he said, slamming the door before his PA could get in.

✳✳✳

"God forbid, I want to get out of here," Garcia said, holding his nostrils.

His PA handed him a scented handkerchief. "I'll go talk to the guard, sir. You can wait here," he said and rushed into the building.

An hour and a half later, Garcia was seated in front of a dingy window, with Mahesh Dube staring at him from the other side. He was handcuffed and his fingers were streaked with dirt. His face was sallow, two weeks having already hollowed out his cheeks to present sharp and angular cheekbones. "Come to gloat?" he said, his voice raspy and unused.

Garcia cocked an eyebrow at him, amused. "Do you want me to gloat? Look where we are at this very moment. Honestly, that's gloating enough, don't you think?"

Mahesh bent forward, his handcuffs noisily hitting the table. "You think you're so funny, don't you? What do you think, just because I'm in here, you can't be? I'm innocent, and you know that."

"Unfortunately, I'm the only one who does."

Mahesh growled. "You ruined my life! Was that your intention all along?" His voice was bordering on a scream. The officer behind him started, but Garcia waved him off. "Was that your intention all along? To kill two birds with one stone? Were you too weak to just fire me to my face?"

At that, Garcia's face lit up. "Oh that! I forgot about that. You're fired. It was almost too easy. The police saw so much more motive once they found out about your past. And CooperCoal is selling, so I guess everything worked out." He chuckled and scraped his chair back to leave.

As he walked away, Mahesh called out. "I'll ruin you. You can't get away with this. You won't."

Garcia turned around and looked him square in the eye. "Watch me."

✳

Anita

In the end, there was no white light. My life didn't flash before my eyes, and I didn't see God, telling me to let go at last. I could feel my mind numbing, as the world began to seep out of the edges of my eyes. There was a fire, ripping at my insides, climbing up and tearing through the back of my throat, as my vision blurred to form the image of my father. He stood tall and straight, looking regal in a suit I'd never seen before.

"You've been so brave," he said, as he reached out to me.

His hand touched my shoulder. I whimpered, as his soothing touch quickly turned into pain, as an electric shock surged through my body with an intensity I could not bear. I tried to scream, but my body had taken over my mind. Everything stopped. I could feel every single cell, every individual nerve ending across my body. I could hear my heartbeat, a dying rhythm, punch out its final calls before that too went still, and for the first time in over two decades, I soared.

Made in the USA
Monee, IL
07 July 2026